ALSO BY EDWARD ST. AUBYN

Never Mind

Bad News

Some Hope

Mother's Milk

At Last

On the Edge

A Clue to the Exit

LOST FOR WORDS

LOST FOR WORDS

EDWARD ST. AUBYN

FARRAR, STRAUS AND GIROUX

NEW YORK

Farrar, Straus and Giroux
18 West 18th Street, New York 10011

Printed in the United States of America
Originally published in 2014 by Picador, an imprint of Pan Macmillan,
Great Britain
Published in the United States by Farrar, Straus and Giroux
First American edition, 2014

Library of Congress Cataloging-in-Publication Data
St. Aubyn, Edward, 1960–
    Lost for words : a novel / Edward St. Aubyn. — First American
edition.
        pages   cm
    ISBN 978-0-374-28029-1 (hardback) — ISBN 978-0-374-71148-1
(ebook)
    1. Novelists—Fiction.   2. Literary prizes—Fiction.   3. Satire.
I. Title.

PR6069.T134 L68 2014
823'.914—dc23
                                                            2013048089

Farrar, Straus and Giroux books may be purchased for educational,
business, or promotional use. For information on bulk purchases,
please contact the Macmillan Corporate and Premium Sales
Department at 1-800-221-7945, extension 5442, or write to
specialmarkets@macmillan.com.

www.fsgbooks.com
www.twitter.com/fsgbooks • www.facebook.com/fsgbooks

1   3   5   7   9   10   8   6   4   2

For Gillon

LOST FOR WORDS

1

When that Cold War relic Sir David Hampshire had approached him about becoming Chair of the Elysian Prize committee, Malcolm Craig asked for twenty-four hours to consider the offer. He had a visceral dislike of Hampshire, the epitome of a public-school mandarin, who had still been Permanent Secretary at the Foreign Office when Malcolm was a new Member of Parliament. After he retired, Hampshire took on the usual bushel of non-executive director-ships that were handed out to people of his kind, including a position on the board of the Elysian Group, where he had somehow fallen into the role of selecting the committees for their literary prize. His breadth of experience and range of contacts were always cited as the justification, but the truth was that David liked power of any sort; the power of influence, the power of money and the power of patronage.

Malcolm's doubts were not confined to Hampshire. Elysian was a highly innovative but controversial agricultural company. It numbered among its products some of the world's most radical herbicides and pesticides, and was a leader in the field of genetically modified crops, crossing wheat with Arctic cod to make it frost resistant, or lemons with bullet ants to give them extra zest. Their Giraffe carrots had been a great help to the busy housewife, freeing her to peel a single carrot for Sunday lunch instead of a whole bunch or bag.

Nevertheless, environmentalists had attacked one Elysian product after another, claiming that it caused cancer, disrupted the food chain, destroyed bee populations, or turned cattle into cannibals. As the noose of British, European and American legislation closed around it, the company had to face the challenge of finding new markets in the less hysterically regulated countries of Africa, Asia and Latin America. That was where the Foreign Office, liaising with Trade and Industry, had stepped in with their combined expertise in exports and diplomacy. The latter had come very much to the fore after some regrettable suicides among Indian farmers, whose crops had failed when they were sold Cod wheat, designed to withstand the icy rigours of Canada and Norway rather than the glowing anvil of the Indian Plain. Although the company disclaimed any responsibility, an unusually generous consignment of Salamander wheat proved such a success that Elysian was able to use a shot of the gratefully waving villagers, their colourful clothing pressed to their elegantly thin bodies by the billows of a departing helicopter, in one of its advertising campaigns.

Elysian's weaponized agricultural agents had come to Malcolm's attention when he was asked to sit on the Government committee responsible for the '*Checkout* List'. Aerially dispersed, *Checkout* caused any vegetation on the ground to burst immediately into flame, forcing enemy soldiers into open country where they could be destroyed by more conventional means. Debates about the *Checkout* List had of course remained secret, and from the general public's point of view, Elysian's name continued to be associated almost entirely with its literary prize.

In the end it was backbench boredom that persuaded Malcolm to accept the chairmanship of the prize committee. An obscure opposition MP needed plenty of extra-curricular activities to secure a decent amount of public attention. Who knew what opportunities his new role might bring? His moment in the pallid Caledonian sun as Under-Secretary of State for Scotland had been the climax of his career so far, as well, he hoped, as the climax of his self-sabotage. He had lost the job by making a reckless speech about Scottish independence that ran directly contrary to his party's official policy and ensured that he would have to resign. He hoped he might one day return to his old job, but for the moment it was time to put away affairs of state and take up childish things, to look through a glass darkly – over a long lunch. When he rang Hampshire to tell him the happy news, he couldn't resist asking why the prize was confined to the Imperial ash heap of the Commonwealth.

'Those are the terms of the endowment,' said Hampshire drily. 'On the wider question of why an institution as vacuous and incoherent as the Commonwealth continues to exist, my answer is this: it gives the Queen some pleasure and that is reason enough to keep it.'

'Well, that's good enough for me,' said Malcolm, waiting tactfully until he had hung up the phone to add, 'you silly old twat.'

Broadly speaking, he did not regret his decision. His secretary was busier than she had been for a good while, collecting newspaper clippings and recordings of radio interviews. Malcolm noticed an increase in the ripple effect of his presence in the Commons bar, and an added liveliness to his conversations at dinner parties. The only aggravating aspect of the process was Hampshire's refusal to consult him about the other members of the committee.

As a well-known columnist and media personality, Jo Cross, the first to be appointed, made sense by raising the public profile of the prize. She turned out to be a veritable geyser of opinions, but once Malcolm managed to make her focus, it turned out that her ruling passion was 'relevance'.

'The question I'll be asking myself as I read a book,' she explained, 'is "just how relevant is this to my readers?"'

'Your readers?' said Malcolm.

'Yes, they're the people I understand, and feel fiercely loyal to. I suppose you would call them my constituents.'

'Thanks for putting that in terms I can easily grasp,' said Malcolm, without showing the patronizing bitch the slightest sign of irony.

The presence of an Oxbridge academic, in the form of Vanessa Shaw, the second recruit, was probably unavoidable. In the last analysis, Malcolm felt there was no harm in having one expert on the history of literature, if it reassured the public. When he invited her to the Commons for tea, she kept saying that she was interested in 'good writing'.

'I'm sure we're all interested in good writing,' said Malcolm, 'but do you have any *special* interest?'

'Especially good writing,' said Vanessa stubbornly.

The committee member Malcolm most resented was one of Hampshire's old girlfriends from the Foreign Office, Penny Feathers. She had neither celebrity nor a distinguished public career to recommend her, and a little Googling soon established the emptiness of Hampshire's claim that she was a 'first-class' author in her own right. Malcolm couldn't look at her without thinking, 'What in God's name are you doing on *my* committee?' He had to remind himself that she had one of five votes and his mission was to make sure that her vote went his way.

The final appointee was an actor Malcolm had never heard of. Tobias Benedict was a godson of Hampshire's who had been 'a fanatical reader ever since he was a little boy'. He missed the first two meetings, due to rehearsals, but sent an effusive apology on a handwritten card, saying that he was there 'in spirit if not in the flesh', that he was reading 'like a madman', and that he was 'in love with' *All the World's a Stage*, a novel Malcolm had not got round to yet. The truth was that he had no intention of reading more than a small proportion of the two hundred novels originally submitted to the committee. His role was to inspire, to guide, to collate and above all, to delegate. In this case, he asked Penny Feathers to look into Tobias's choice, feeling that one lame duck should investigate another.

He asked his secretary to skim through the early submissions looking for his own special interest, anything with a Scottish flavour. She had come up with three novels of which he had so far only had time to look at one. A harsh but ultimately uplifting account of life on a Glasgow housing estate, *wot u starin at* really hit the spot when it came to new voices, the real concerns of ordinary people, and the dark underbelly of the Welfare State. He intended to lend it his support and start a discreet campaign on its behalf. He was also pleased, for personal reasons, that she had unearthed *The Greasy Pole*, a novel by Alistair

Mackintosh, but he must be careful not to support it too overtly.

When it came to running a committee, Malcolm favoured a collegiate approach: there was nothing like proving you were a team player to get your own way. The point was to build a consensus and come up with a vision of the sort of Britain they all wanted to project with the help of this prize: diverse, multi-cultural, devolutionary, and of course, encouraging to young writers. After all, young writers were the future, or at any rate, would be the future – if they were still around and being published. You couldn't go wrong with the future. Even if it was infused with pessimism, until it was compromised by the inevitable cross-currents of unexpected good news and character-building opportunities, the pessimism remained perfect, unsullied by that much more insidious and dangerous quality, disappointment. The promise of young writers was perfect as well, until they burnt out, fucked up or died – but that would be under another government and under another committee.

2

Sam Black had written nothing that day. He was too preoccupied with the psychological contracts under which he had been allowed to write so far. What were they and could they be changed?

One contract was Faustian, in a secular and internalized version, but Faustian nevertheless. Haunted by the threat of madness and the consequent need to commit suicide, the modern Faustian was under an obligation to write in order to save his life. Damnation was the hell of his own depression, with a boutique Mephistopheles no longer offering infinite knowledge and worldly power, but the more modest sublimatory power of a practice that might one day release the artist from the destructive forces raging in his psyche.

Sam also recognized that his writing was an ingenious decoy, drawing attention away from his own decaying body towards a potentially immaculate body of work. He named this deflection the 'Hephaestus complex', as if it had always been part of the annals of psychoanalysis. His angry father Zeus threw Hephaestus out of Olympus when he took his mother's side in a parental argument. Hephaestus's fall shattered his leg and made him lame, but the people of Lemnos, the island where he landed, took him in and taught him to be a master craftsman. Living under Mount Etna, using the volcano as his furnace, he became the disfigured fire god who made beautiful artefacts, and was given the most beautiful goddess, Aphrodite, as his wife. Even when she cuckolded him, he used art to avenge his pain and captured her with Aries in an unbreakable but invisibly fine net from which the adulterous couple could not escape.

Orpheus was an inevitable member of this gang of ancient enforcers. The man who sang his way out of hell only to let slip the woman he had gone there to retrieve was the world expert on haunting loss that every *artiste maudit* had to sign up with. His clinging melancholy was punished with decapitation, but even when his severed head was floating downriver, it continued to sing of Eurydice.

At first Sam had wanted to purge himself of these psychological contracts through a meticulous negativity. Like a man walking backwards along a path, erasing his footsteps with a broom, he had tried, through contradiction, negation, paradox, unreliable narration and every other method he could devise, to cancel the tracks left by his words and to release his writing from the wretched positivity of affirming anything at all. He hoped that by stripping all forms of belief from his sentences, he could evacuate his cluttered mind, leaving it empty and clear. Appearances were disappearances in the making – not that disappearances weren't appearances as well, otherwise the disappearance would have the retroactive effect of solidifying what disappeared, an obvious mistake. Nothing could hold him or trap him – except his belief that freedom could be achieved by simply refusing to be held or trapped.

When his sceptical texts could find no publisher, he was frustrated. He wanted to achieve enough to know, and not just to assume, that achievement was an alluring and arduous dead end. And so Sam put the typescript of *False Notes* in a box on top of the cupboard in his bedroom, and submitted to the grim rule of Faustus, Orpheus and Hephaestus, writing his first published novel, a *bildungsroman* of impeccable anguish and undisguised autobiographical origin. He knew that his publishers had high hopes for *The Frozen Torrent*, and he joined them in hoping that it would make it to the Elysian Short List so that he could re-submit *False Notes* and finally win his freedom from the tyranny of pain-based art.

These grave considerations were not the only things distracting Sam from his work. He also found it impossible to let more than a few seconds elapse without thinking of Katherine Burns. She was famously easy to fall in love with. He had been waiting throughout February for her return from India. Today she had finally written to him from Delhi, saying that when she got back she would be working flat out to make the Elysian deadline, but inviting him for a drink the week after Easter.

If only she didn't live with her publisher. Sam disliked having his passion tainted by jealousy. He had nothing against Alan Oaks personally – he hardly knew him, and in any case Alan was relentlessly friendly – it was more of a geographical objection: how dare he lie next to her in bed?

There was something rather French about the way Katherine surrounded herself with artists, thinkers, scientists and writers, like an old-fashioned *salon-nière*, if not in an *enfilade* of double-doored white and gold rooms in the rue du Bac, at least in her Bayswater flat, with books in the window sill and books on the floor. She only seemed to have affairs with men who were twenty years older than her (although she liked women of her own age) and he worried that without a sex change, he might simply be too young. She commanded unwavering devotion from her lovers, in a way that reminded him of a certain species of wasp that paralysed its prey without killing it, so as to assure its offspring a supply of living flesh; but he knew that he was just defending himself from rejection with these dark fantasies. The truth was she was utterly wonderful and he adored her.

3

'I enjoyed my time at the University in Delhi,'
said Sonny, over the rattle of the ineffective air
conditioning. 'We used to loll about in any sort of
costume, ragging each other and making plans for
pleasure trips.'

His eyelids, which had been drooping from the
recollection of those languid days, suddenly shot
open.

'And then,' he said, leaning towards Katherine
with a troubled look, 'the vimin arrived.'

'The what?' said Katherine.

'The vimin,' repeated Sonny. He sank back again,
trying to dismiss the painful memory with a swipe of
his wrist. 'Everyone started rushing about – brushing
their teeth.'

Sonny closed his eyes, shutting out that rush of

fools, and the rush of years that now separated him from those days. He was immediately consoled by the knowledge that he had redeemed all that seemingly wasted time with his magnum opus, *The Mulberry Elephant*. He was also enjoying the delicious irony that Katherine Burns, who was considered to be a tip-top novelist, had no idea that she was in the presence of a literary genius who outweighed her in every respect.

Mum was the word for the moment. When *Mulberry* appeared on the Elysian Long List, he would fly over to England. The interviews would begin when he was Short Listed, and after his inevitable triumph was announced at the Elysian Dinner, he would deliver the witty and magnanimous acceptance speech he had already sketched out a dozen times. 'I want to thank the judges for their enlightened decision. Enlightenment is something we Indians know a thing or two about, but tonight it's England's turn . . .' He imagined the shudder of laughter breaking out in the Banqueting Room of the illustrious Fishmongers' Hall. He would be encouraging to the lesser talents, and humble in the face of greatness.

Katherine watched Sonny murmuring to himself. He was reclining on silk cushions in the corner of a frantically carved daybed, his legs tucked towards him, a slender hand clasping one of his ankles. She could see his eyes swivelling under their lids in a way that reminded her of the rapid eye movement of a dreamer, as well as the ceaseless vigilance of the blind. A pair of yellow slippers idled on the carpet. Two turbaned servants were placing dozens of silver pots onto the engraved silver table in the middle of the room. Her throne of castellated mahogany, too deep to sit back in and too jagged to lean against, made her long to leave.

She wished she hadn't asked Didier to call Sonny before she left England. Like all her ex-lovers, except for the occasional Spartacus who would lead a gallant but futile revolt, easily crushed by a friendly email or a chance encounter, Didier remained her slave. If only he had been a little more reluctant to get in touch with his grand Indian acquaintance. He hadn't seen Sonny for ten years and he warned Katherine that she would find him 'exotique, but totally crazy'. Before leaving England 'totally crazy' seemed a fair price for 'exotique', but after three weeks of travelling in India she felt the opposite. Tonight, thank God, she was flying back to the welcome dullness of London in early March.

Sonny's head turned as if synchronized with the arrival of the elderly woman in a maroon and gold sari who now stood in the doorway.

'Auntie!' said Sonny, rising from the daybed. 'May I present Katherine Burns, she's a lady novelist from London.'

'Oh, how delightful,' said Auntie and then, noticing that Katherine hadn't moved, she added, 'Don't get up, my dear, nobody curtsies any more these days; or only the old stick in the muds,' her voice filled with mock-horror at the mention of this category. 'We're just having a cosy little lunch, nothing formal.'

She sat on the edge of the daybed and toyed with the folds of her sari.

'You're just the person I need,' she began, conscious of the favour she was doing Katherine. 'I've written the most marvellous cookery book – full of family portraits – and, of course, recipes that have been handed down from generation to generation by the cooks at the old palace.' She hurried over this detail as if it were hardly worth mentioning. 'You're in the publishing world, could you take one of the manuscripts back with you and place it with a London publisher for me? We used to know the great

English writers, Somerset Maugham and dear old Paddy Leigh Fermor, but they all seem to be dead now, or out of commission. So, you see, my dear, I'm relying on you.'

'Of course,' said Katherine, trying to assemble a smile.

4

Over the last few weeks, Penny had been so preoccupied by becoming a member of the Elysian Prize committee that she had neglected her own writing, but she was determined to get back to work on her current thriller, *Roger and Out*. She clicked, a little nervously, on its icon and found herself confronted by sentences she hadn't looked at for ages. To give herself a running jump, she re-read the beginning of the latest chapter.

It was evening in St James's Park and the sun, sinking in a westerly direction, had turned the clouds into pink balls of cotton wool. Meanwhile, at ground level, the puddles had already turned into dark pools of glossy chocolate.

Sitting in her battered grey Audi A6 3.0 litre TDI

with all leather seats, Jane Street was ready to call it a day. That was the surveillance game for you, waiting and watching, watching and waiting, but often ending up with nothing to show for it. Then, just as Jane's hand came to rest on the ignition key, Grove's voice blasted into her earpiece.

'I have an eyeball. I have an eyeball.'

The words shot through Jane's body like an electric current. She reached instinctively into the Audi's generous glove compartment and felt for her weapon. The IPX370 packed the punch of a Colt .38, but its magazine carried that one extra bullet that could make all the difference if things turned nasty. Six grams shy of its American counterpart, its lighter weight also made a real difference if you had to carry it round in your handbag all day.

Jane's hand padded around the glove compartment, but apart from the service manual and a spare packet of Handy Andies, she could feel nothing there. Where the hell was her weapon? Then it all came back with a cold sickening thud. The shooting range. That morning. Richard Lane. Lane was a classic yes-man and pen-pusher, with no more idea of the reality of life at the sharp end of things than she had of how to dance the lead role in Tchaikovsky's Swan

Lake. Probably less. She had been avoiding Lane like the plague, but he had finally tracked her down at the shooting range and delivered his usual lecture about her 'cavalier disregard for the proper rules of procedure', her 'run-away expenses' and her 'attitude generally'. It had made her so angry that she had left her weapon behind. She had spent the whole afternoon fuming and hadn't had a chance to discover her mistake. Now it was too late.

Well, damn Lane, damn all the Lanes, sitting behind their desks in Thames House, watching the shafts of sunlight turn the river lapis lazuli, while their love-sick secretaries made bookings for lunch at Quo Vadis in Soho's Dean Street. What did they know about putting your life on the line for your country?

Penny was torn between thinking that the pages were rather good – pacey, well researched, vivid – and thinking that she was not really a writer at all. Perhaps it had been a huge mistake to retire early from the Foreign Office to pursue her lifelong ambition of becoming an author. It was true that there had been other reasons to leave. Her career had stagnated after its dazzlingly rapid rise during David Hampshire's last years as Permanent Secretary, over twenty-five years ago. His favouritism had generated so much resentment that she remained stuck at the same level ever after, often moving sideways but never up. Her affair with David not only ruined her marriage, but arguably ruined her prospects as well. He was still her greatest friend, but the glory days were over, when he used to call her 'my very own Anna Ford', at a time when the nation's favourite newscaster was considered the most desirable woman on Earth. Unlike the delicious Miss Ford, who had confidently allowed her hair to go white, Penny's remained resolutely mahogany, matching her eyes, but increasingly at odds with the sad story told by the sags and creases of her loosening skin. Penny sighed. Nicola had never really forgiven her for the divorce – or, if it came to that, for the career – but she wasn't going to think about that now; she must press on, if only to get away from the old feelings of hollow sacrifice that she fought against every day.

'Damascus is on the bridge. Damascus is crossing the bridge,' said Grove's audibly tense voice. 'Where the hell are you, Street?'

Jane closed the glove compartment. She was about

to *face Ibrahim al-Shukra, one of the world's most dangerous and ruthless men, responsible for the horrific, cowardly, tragic and completely uncalled for deaths of countless innocent members of the public, and she was unarmed.*

'Damascus has stopped on the bridge.' Grove was audibly relieved. 'Damascus is feeding the ducks.'

'I'm on my way,' said Jane.

'Roger that,' said Grove.

Well, Jane reflected philosophically, she may not have the reassuring weight of the IPX370 in her hand, but she still had her handbag (it wouldn't be the first time she'd used that as a weapon), her common sense and, above all, her professionalism.

The word 'professionalism' stung Penny with guilt about the previous night. She was meant to be baby-sitting for Nicola, but had quite simply forgotten until it was too late. Nicola had always reproached Penny for being a neglectful mother, and now she was going to have 'neglectful grandmother' added to the list of her crimes. Whatever her daughter might think, when push came to shove, she had a strong maternal side. Nevertheless, she was the first to admit that public service had taken the lion's share of her attention. Nicola had become a latchkey kid, travelling on the Underground to school at an early age, letting herself in and making her own tea, putting herself to bed, booking her own holidays and going off with other families to unknown foreign destinations. It hadn't been ideal, but at least it had helped to make the her independent.

The night before Nicola had been planning to see *Chitty Chitty Bang Bang*, a ritual she repeated on the anniversary of the occasion that Penny had promised to take her but had been forced to let her down. President Reagan had just invaded Grenada, or at least sent some Marines to invade Grenada, and Penny had felt that she simply had to stay at her desk to help draft the Foreign Office response. Even then she had been a writer, although a team of specialists handled the actual wording.

Penny couldn't help wincing from the memory of last night's telephone call to Nicola.

'Don't worry, darling, I'm on my way,' she reassured Nicola when she suddenly remembered what she was supposed to be doing.

'Don't fucking bother,' Nicola shouted. 'I'm going to miss the show again anyway.'

'I don't know if it's escaped your notice,' said Penny, 'but I'm part of the team that's been put in charge of English Literature this year and, whether you like it or not, that's a pretty big responsibility.'

'Oh, piss off,' said Nicola and hung up.

Penny's own childhood had taken place during the Second World War. Her earliest memory was of sitting in her nursery one afternoon, playing with her favourite toy, a lovely doll's house with a pretty red and white chequered tablecloth in its kitchen, and a little kitten sitting curled up by the fire in the living room. Suddenly, with a dreadful screeching sound, a hole appeared in the floor only a few inches from where she was sitting, and her doll's house disappeared. A bomb had dropped straight onto her house, ripping through the roof, the nursery, her parents' bedroom, the dining room, and finally getting lodged in the basement, unexploded.

Nowadays that would mean instant counselling, but in wartime Britain you picked yourself up, avoiding the gaping hole in the middle of the room, and carried on. And what's more, you remembered to count your blessings. Yes, there was an unexploded bomb in the foundations of your childhood home, undermining its rental value and putting your parents under considerable financial strain, but you never forgot that if there was one thing worse than an unexploded bomb, it was a bomb that *did* explode.

All her life Penny felt that showing emotion was a sign of weakness. Emotions were what other people were allowed to have. She was there to help, and although she might not have all the answers, or even a very clear idea of what people were talking about when they talked about their feelings, she could make sure that the kettle was on, or the gin and tonic ready to hand, so that things would start to look better for those who were struggling.

Penny scrolled down to her latest paragraph. She wanted to get at least a thousand words written before lunch. But she was also determined to shake off her dependency on some highly addictive software called Ghost and the two ambitions might be hard to reconcile.

At the beginning of her trilogy, Penny had liked basic Ghost so much that she went on to buy Gold Ghost and Gold Ghost Plus. When you typed in a word, 'refugee' for instance, several useful suggestions popped up: 'clutching a pathetic bundle', or 'eyes big with hunger'; for 'assassin' you got 'ice water running through his veins', and 'his eyes were cold narrow slits'. Under 'shoes' you got 'badly scuffed', 'highly polished', 'seen better days', and 'bought in Paris'. If you typed 'river' into Gold Ghost Plus, you got 'dark flood flecked with gold', or 'wearing her evening gown of fiery silk'. When you looked up 'thought', you found 'food for' and 'perish the'. She could scroll and click, scroll and click all day, with the word count going up in leaps and bounds.

She found herself getting weekly crushes on writing tricks of one sort or another: cricket metaphors, when everyone started playing with a straight bat, or dropping an easy catch; or it was descriptions of the weather that set her imagination on fire, and clouds appeared in the sky like 'big sponges', or covered cities like 'a wet blanket'. Her word of the week last week had been 'imperceptibly'. One of her characters had 'glanced imperceptibly', while another had 'imperceptibly moved her hand'. The action had generally taken on an imperceptible air, which set it apart from a run of the mill thriller.

Roger and Out was the third volume of her trilogy. When all was said and done, the first volume, *Follow That Car*, had been tepidly received, but the sequel, *Roger That*, secured a smashing review in the *Daily Express*. She had the key quote, '*Feathers knows her stuff*', blown up, framed and hanging in the guest loo of her cottage in Suffolk. She sometimes had a funny feeling when she realized that she would soon be parted from the characters she'd been living with all these months. Was it sadness? She wasn't sure, but whatever it was, she wasn't going to dwell on it.

5

Didier's arm was looped over Katherine's shoulder, one hand spread across her still-pounding heart, the other cupped over the hard curve of her navel ring.

Didier wondered again if there was not something excessive, something obscene, about his enjoyment of Katherine's body. Once its material desires had been satisfied, commodity fetishism moved on to amorous and spiritual dimensions. He was living, engulfed by a mental fog analogous to religious fervour, in a late capitalist utopia of obligatory permissiveness, with its injunction to gratify ever more perverse desires.

'What does it mean when we say . . .' Didier began.

'Shhh,' said Katherine. Half her motive for sex was to let her mind fall silent. Didier's compulsion to talk, to analyse everything, to live in a perpetual semiotic frenzy, was one of the reasons their affair had been so brief. She also didn't want Didier to think that they were having a general revival. She was just dealing with the emergency, or taking advantage of the opportunity, it was hard to know which, of Alan's absence. They had worked hard on editing her novel when she got back from India and then he had gone to a conference in Guttenberg on the future of the book. For him that counted as work, but she was left dangerously unemployed.

Shhh, she must stop as well. She had only just finished making love and she was already chattering. She thought of an empty train shooting through an empty station at night, an image of her mind without words. How beautifully unnecessary they seemed at that moment, but soon it would be rush hour, with hardly enough words getting off the crowded train to allow any words from the crowded platform to get on. Everything congested with words, everything spoken for; conversations, dialogues, monologues, interior monologues, all the way down, words staining the marrow, pretending that nothing existed without them. She almost wanted to make love again to get back to silence, but Sam was coming for a drink in half an hour, with the inevitable punctuality of a lovesick man. She must get ready.

Complacencies of the peignoir, or power shower: which word cluster would get her?

'Okay, I get up now,' said Didier, taking control of his rejection, pushing aside the bedclothes and picking up his shirt from the floor.

She gave him what he wanted, rolling over and raising herself enough to lean against his back.

'That was so nice,' she said, kissing him on his shoulder.

'What does it mean that I'm your ex-lover when I have just come inside you?' said Didier.

'It means you got lucky,' said Katherine.

'Maybe I get lucky again,' said Didier, turning towards her and lunging with his mouth.

Katherine allowed herself to be kissed.

'I have a friend coming in twenty minutes,' she said, with regret and impatience.

'The next man!' said Didier. '*Fais attention!* One day air-traffic control goes on strike and there is a terrible accident!'

'You can stay, if you like.'

'I'm sorry, but voyeurism is not my taste,' said Didier.

'He's just a friend,' she said, getting off the bed and switching on the bathroom light. Katherine was bored by jealousy; she had been bombarded by so much of it, there hadn't been time to find out if she had any of her own.

'What does it mean, this superposition of two impossible categories: lover / ex-lover . . .'

Katherine turned on the shower, missing the conclusion of Didier's penetrating enquiry. By the time she got out, he was fully clothed and sitting in the armchair in the corner of her bedroom.

'It creates the space of pure paradox, like the ephemeral emergence of a particle from the quantum vacuum – the vacuum which is *not* a vacuum!'

'Sorry, but have you been talking while I was in the shower, or did you just start up again when I came out?' she asked.

'In the end, what difference does it make?' said Didier.

'Well, if I missed a chunk, that might explain why I have no idea what you're talking about,' she said, letting her towel drop to the ground.

Didier fell silent.

'*Putain*,' he finally managed, after she had stepped into her knickers. 'This is what it is like to be Actaeon:

you know that you will be torn apart by the hunting dogs, but you don't care!'

'I don't think he did know,' said Katherine, emerging from her T-shirt.

'Of course he didn't know!' said Didier. 'But *we* know, because we do not live in the myth, but in the *knowledge* of the myth. Evidently, the collective unconscious has become the collective self-conscious!'

The doorbell rang.

'Just in time,' said Katherine, doing up the button on her jeans. 'I mean I got my jeans on just in time.'

'Do not worry,' said Didier, following her into the hall. 'My narcissism is not offended, in fact it may be gratified by the idea that this interruption was "just in time" to save you from my theories!'

'Hi, Sam,' said Katherine to the hazy image on her entryphone, pressing the buzzer to let him in.

'You pay me the compliment of resistance,' Didier continued. 'There can be no resistance without the fear of penetration!'

Katherine took Didier's head in her hands and gave him a long slow kiss, knowing that even he had to stop talking while her tongue was in his mouth. She only broke away when there was a knock on the door.

'And so you penetrate me instead,' Didier concluded triumphantly.

Sam could tell that Katherine had just been in bed with Didier. Her hair was wet from the shower and he smelt ostentatiously of sex. Sam also knew that the grey-haired Frenchman was not supposed to be her current lover. Her openness to infidelity filled him with an optimism that her choice of infidelity discouraged.

Katherine introduced the rivalrous men and took them through to the drawing room. An image flashed across her mind of two rams flinging their heads against each other on a rocky mountainside. What did the girl rams do? Faint with pleasure? Clap their cloven hooves? Lean against some nearby boulders, with little tubs of mountain grass, discussing the battle?

'So you got your novel in before the deadline,' said Sam.

'Yes,' said Katherine, wondering what it would be like to go to bed with both of them at once.

'Ah, yes,' said Didier. 'The famous Elysian. In France we have the Concour. It is *completely* corrupt, and for that reason the rules are absolutely clear. That is the paradox of corruption: it is much more legalistic than the law! But this Elysian, *c'est du pur casino.*'

'I have an idea,' said Katherine, determined to go ahead now that Didier had started talking. 'Perhaps we should have a drink first.'

6

Although he could see almost nothing through his dark glasses, Sonny felt that he needed their protection against the phosphorescent ocean of clicking and flashing *paparazzi* that might well be churning restlessly, somewhere beyond passport control, awaiting his arrival. The gutter press would only be doing its vulgar and familiar work, feeding an insatiable public with images of an Indian grandee who had stooped to conquer English Letters with his masterwork, *The Mulberry Elephant*. He understood their hunger and was modestly dressed for the occasion. He had just squeezed back into the slate-grey raw-silk frock coat that the pretty little air hostess fetched for him from the First Class cupboard. Underneath his frock coat, he wore a long pale-peach shirt and loose white trousers, pinched at the ankle and finished off with a pair of his signature yellow slippers. As he left his seat, he draped his shoulder, carelessly but perfectly, with a folded beige shawl of a surpassing softness that could only be achieved by weaving together the almost non-existent hairs of several hundred unborn Kashmiri mountain goats. He had one of the genuine pre-war articles, not one of these fake things they sold on every street corner in Paris and Milano.

His shawl was not only proof against England's loutish climate, it also spared him from contact with objects, like doorknobs and light switches, that could have been handled by almost anybody; murderers and butchers, moneylenders and lavatory attendants. It could also be called upon to wrap around materials abhorrent to his sensitive touch, like the slippery, effeminate plastic used in plastic bags.

For the first fourteen years of his life he had never even set eyes on a plastic bag. Confined to the palace and its magnificent grounds, more varied and luxuriant than the Botanical Gardens of Kew, filled with peacocks and cockatoos and herds of antelope, he would ride around with his tutors and his equerry and the rest of his entourage, one day on an elephant, the next in a pony and trap, never seeing other children and seldom seeing his parents, but wanting for nothing among all the delightful follies and spectacles arranged for his entertainment; the orchestras that struck up as he rounded a corner, or the famous battles re-enacted for his birthday. On an island in the middle of the Home Lake, a sadhu had been persuaded to take up residence under a baobab tree. With his body covered in ash and hair down to his waist, he meditated all day with imperturbable concentration. Sonny's tutor encouraged him to test the holy man's resolve by emptying baskets full of harmless grass snakes over his head, or setting fire to his loin cloth, only putting it out at the very last moment. What fun they had! And yet one day, when Sonny was fourteen, as he was galloping around his private racecourse, after winning yet another race against the Household Jockeys, he was suddenly overcome by a longing to go beyond the palace gates and see the city, which sometimes betrayed its presence as a faint smudge in the air, complicating the glorious sunsets which were such a talking point among guests at the palace. His father had forbidden him to leave the grounds, and Sonny spent many weeks planning his secret expedition and accumulating what he imagined was an appropriate disguise in which to move unnoticed among his people.

When he finally arrived at the outskirts of the city, he wrapped his borrowed garments more tightly around himself, cupping his palm over his nostrils to filter the stagnant air, clogged with the thick odours of cooking, the stench of sewage and the reek of rotting marigolds. He finally emerged from the miserable maze of leprous lanes, their mud walls plastered with drying cow dung and streaked with crimson eructations of betel juice, and found himself on open ground overlooking the river. Back at the palace the melting spring snows were artfully channelled into fountains and bathing pools, into swift streams whose murmuring music enlivened shaded pleasure grounds; here, beside the city, the sluggish flood burnt in the sun like molten glass, its unlovely banks strewn with garbage. Somewhere down by the glaring water he could hear the crackle of a funeral pyre. Slipping on the dark glasses which, mercifully, he had tucked into his shirt pocket at the last moment, Sonny watched as a blackened corpse, excruciated by the intense heat, sat up for the last time, while a pariah dog gnawed on a charred limb that had escaped the flames and lay smoking on the greasy beach. Further along the shore, an indifferent washerwoman beat clothes on a rock and chucked them into a tub nearby.

Shaking off these memories as he moved towards the exit, Sonny nodded at the cluster of air hostesses, accepting their longing to see him again on board their airline as the inevitable consequence of the awe that he inspired. One of them, not completely ignorant of the history and traditions of her country, must have known and then told the others, in a lather of excitement, that the passenger in the front row (he had, as usual, reserved the entire front row, so as not to find himself sitting next to that famous bore, God-Knows-Who) was the six hundred and fifty-third maharaja of Badanpur. Sonny could trace his ancestry, according to the highest Brahminical authority, back to Krishna, the dark-blue god. The thought of those happy days when gods had mingled freely with humankind, and infused his own lineage with divinity, brought a radiant smile to Sonny's face, as if he were Krishna himself, smiling at the exquisite milkmaid who was to become the first great Queen and Founding Mother of the House of Badanpur. Sonny saw the pretty little girl who had fetched his frock coat stagger for a moment, as if trying to regain her balance after an obscure shock wave that only he could fully understand had passed through the cabin. He almost reached out to support her, but checked his compassion, feeling that his touch might have the opposite effect, throwing this frail human creature to the ground and robbing her of her sanity, like a circuit incinerated by a charge that it was never designed to carry.

As he sped through Heathrow's long low corridors in a beeping golf cart, Sonny checked his phone to see if Katherine Burns had sent a text, shedding light on the mystery of *The Mulberry Elephant* having so far received no notices in the British press. He didn't pretend to understand the workings of a newspaper editor's mind, but he could imagine that the press would want to make a bigger splash by synchronizing all the profiles, reviews, interviews, television chat shows, and guest appearances in popular soap operas, with the explosive appearance of *Mulberry* on the Elysian Big List. The more he thought about it, the more obvious it was that there could be no other explanation, but he was disappointed, if not altogether surprised, that Miss Burns was so overcome with professional jealousy that she was unable to tell him herself. He had only received one communication from her, a scratchy postcard thanking him for lunch, at least a month too late, and saying that she had given Auntie's cookbook to her publisher, but that it was a crowded market and not to raise her hopes too high.

At the UK Border, an absurd little man asked Sonny the purpose of his visit. When Sonny said that he had come two weeks ahead of the Big List, so as to be thoroughly well rested before the hullabaloo of the publicity circus, the little man asked him what exactly this publicity would be for.

'My novel, of course,' said Sonny.

'So, you've come to the UK to promote a novel,' said the man.

'I have come to accept congratulations for my novel,' said Sonny impatiently. 'I have nothing to do with trade.'

'Is the novel published in the UK?'

'No!' said Sonny. 'It is published in India – privately!'

'So you are in fact trying to promote and sell goods from India in the UK,' concluded his tormentor, 'but on your Immigration Form you ticked the box stating that the purpose of your trip is pleasure.'

'The purpose of my entire existence is pleasure,' said Sonny angrily, 'but I can't say that I'm experiencing any at the moment!'

He had perhaps been unwise to lose his temper. He spent the next four hours in a depressing cubicle talking to one grim example after another of the bureaucratic breed. When he showed them his four First Class return tickets, and a phone call to Claridge's confirmed that he'd booked the Arnold Bennett Suite for the next month, they reluctantly admitted him to the country, but spitefully limited his visit to twenty days, giving him only five days after the Big List. To think that his ancestors had already spent millennia being cooled by rose sherbets and peacock fans, while these fellows were still prancing around on frigid beaches, dressed in rotting animal skins, and jabbering away in the rudiments of a language it had fallen on him to raise to the highest level of art, brought him close to hysteria, but by the time he was reclining in the back of the Claridge's car, massaging his temples, the calm waters of luxury and destiny started to close over the ripples of mere circumstance, and he decided that he would indeed leave the country in twenty days, at his own instigation, in order to spend an amusing night in Le Touquet, or Deauville, returning to England the next day, in the reasonable expectation that on this occasion the border would not be guarded by a *complete madman*.

7

As Vanessa looked up from her armchair and stared out at the quad, the pale-honey stone of the college chapel and the leaded diamonds of its window-panes lit up in a burst of sunlight, and then darkened again. She imagined the scudding spring clouds she couldn't see; she noticed the invitation from the brief shift of light to transcend and then reclaim her overburdened mood. She accepted and put aside all these mental operations and felt restored, after only a few moments of lucid daydreaming, to a salutary independence of mind in which she could place her attention where she chose, with little interference from her emotions and her surroundings.

She was doing what she was paid to do: being intelligent about writing. Rather too much writing, it was true. In just over an hour her first-year students would be coming to read their essays on 'Evil in the Brontës'. As usual, none of them would have read *Villette*. She had eight essays to mark before tomorrow on the Metaphysical poets. ('Yoked by violence together' – was Dr Johnson right? They would all say no, of course, and quote T. S. Eliot on Donne.) The second draft of a PhD thesis on the history of the semi-colon, which Vanessa had recklessly agreed to supervise, would have to wait until Saturday. Sunday was earmarked for her own book on Edith Wharton's Women. The trouble was that on Sunday she and Stephen had to go and see Poppy in the clinic. Poppy was back inside after her weight dropped below thirty-five kilos. The slightest hint that her mother was in a hurry to get back to work would be treated by Poppy as further evidence of betrayal and neglect, of Vanessa's preference for ideas over human relationships, of an academic ambition whose impossibly high standards were ultimately responsible for her illness. Poppy's eating disorder had started during the term before her GCSEs. She later explained, or made up the explanation, that she felt she was not only competing with all the students in her year, but also with her donnish parents, who took her success for granted and only paid attention to her failures. Later, when she did her A-levels, she won a scholarship to Cambridge, where both her parents taught. On the other hand, she had to be admitted to hospital for the first time that year. In support of her argument, it was true that this crisis secured her far more parental attention and professions of love than she had ever been given before.

As Vanessa's mind approached the black hole of her daughter's illness, it tended to veer off into generalizations: the paradox that the inflated exam grades designed to banish low self-esteem from the national psyche made anything less than ten A*s into a source of low self-esteem; the fact that the long backward look now taken by universities encouraged an emphasis on obedience and conformity that were not necessarily the best indicators of intellectual curiosity and incisiveness. She took refuge in the platitudes of her social circle, so much easier to contemplate than her children's individual cases. Tom had returned from the 'birthday party' he had been to last weekend, admitting that it had in fact been an ayahuasca ceremony that ended when one of the participants went into a coma. With only eight weeks before his A-levels, Tom had spent three days at home recovering from the weekend's psychedelic ordeal. Now that Poppy was back in the clinic, Vanessa had lost her nerve and instead of lecturing him, carried bowls of soup to his bedroom on a tray.

Quite apart from this multitude of obligations, she was surrounded by the Elysian Prize submissions, piled up around her armchair. These required an immediate and decisive focus, not only to reclaim some floor space by clearing out the hopeless cases (she thought involuntarily of Poppy's bed at the clinic being liberated by her death) but also to get down, over the next two weeks, to the final twenty books out of which the Long List of twelve would then be chosen. Her first task, which she intended to dispatch before the Brontë tutorials, was to take a look at one of Malcolm's candidates, *wot u starin at*. She was inclined to stay on good terms with Malcolm and to keep her polemical powder dry for the later stages of the competition. Her intention was not to read the book through, unless it became a candidate for the Long List, but to let it through, if at all possible, to the last twenty.

She started reading the first page.

'*Fuck! Fuck! Fuck!*'
Death Boy's troosers were round his ankies. The

only vein in his body that hadna bin driven into hiding was in his cock.

'I told yuz nivir ivir to talk to uz when Aym trackin a vein,' snarled Death Boy.

'That way I needna fucking talk ta ya at all,' said Wanker, slumped in the corner, weirdly fascinated by the sour stench of his own vomit, rising off of his soiled Iggy Pop tee-shirt. He was fixed ta the corner, as if some cunt with a nail gun had shot him through the hands and feet and crucified the sorry bastard to Death Boy's floor. Deep in the despair a kenning that he coudna move in any direction, he pissed himself, feeling the warm flood fill his troosers, and at the same time evacuating his tormented bowels, with a mixture a relief, and a touch a pride at the thought that heed be leavin Death Boy's gaff in an even worse state than heed found it. No easy matter.

'Shite,' he whispered with a voice that seemed to come from a thousand miles away and belong to another creature, not necessarily human.

'Awright!' said Death Boy, his face twisted in a kinda sweet hatred. 'Awright! Ay got it, Ay fucking got it, Ay fucking hit the vein. Awright . . .' His words trailed off as the skag came on and he climbed outta the refrigerator where heed bin cramped, naked *and shivering, and stepped out, inta the heat o tha midday sun, and his aching ole bones and bruised ole muscles melted like wax in a fire.*

'That's fuckin awright, that is,' he croaked.

What was so typical of an untrained reader like Malcolm was the claim that this was a work of 'gritty social realism', when in fact it was a piece of surrealistic satire. Vanessa decided to sample another passage from the middle of the book.

'Wot u starin at?' sais the red-haired cunt at the bar.

'Ay wasna starin at anythin,' sais Death Boy.

'Listen, mate,' sais Wanker, who wasna in the mood for a fight, being skag-sick, and pissed at the world on account of his AIDS test comin back positive, 'there's nae cunt staring at nae cunt.'

'Well, you can stare a this,' sais the red-head cunt, and he brings his beer mug down on Death Boy's heid, splitting his skull open.

Death Boy's goat more blood pouring outa him than a pig in an abattoir, only he's so outa his box, he dunna ken he's goat any cause for complaint until he's licked up a good half pint o it.

*Wanker, seeing that a fight is unavoidable, snorts
a line a speed off the bar, goes up to the red-haired
cunt and head-butts him, breakin the fucker's nose.
While the cunt is still trying to get his balance,
Wanker whips out his syringe and sinks it into the
cunt's neck.*

*'Welcome to tha world a AIDS, you psycho cunt,'
sais Wanker.*

*'That's enough of that,' sais the weasel-faced
barman, 'we're no havin any fightin in here. This is a
respectable pub.'*

Yes, well, there it was, thought Vanessa: eighty or
perhaps ninety thousand words of that sort of thing.
An art based on impact, rather than process, structure
or insight, doomed to the jack-hammer monotony of
having to shock again and again. She placed it reluctantly on the stack reserved for the final twenty. She
would let Malcolm have it, for what she was ashamed
to admit were essentially political reasons, but she
would advance her literary objections strongly when
the time came – and when she had read it.

So far the only book she wholeheartedly admired
was *The Frozen Torrent* by Sam Black. It had what
she wanted to call an experience of literature built

into it, an inherent density of reflection on the medium in which it took place: the black backing that makes the mirror shine.

There was a knock on the door. Three minutes early. How keen they were to tell her how many cruelties they had spotted in *Wuthering Heights*, like children bringing pebbles back from the shoreline to distract their parents when they were trying to read.

8

Alan Oaks had managed to catch an earlier flight than expected, and he texted Katherine from the Gatwick Express to tell her the good news. He longed to be with her again, and although he knew his back wasn't up to it, pictured himself sweeping aside the keys and the envelopes from the hall table and having her right there, too impatient to make it as far as the bedroom. By the time he was at the front of the taxi queue, he had compromised realistically and settled on the armchair in the drawing room. With her legs hooked over its arms, she was lowering herself . . .

'Oh, Craven Hill Gardens, please.'

There had been opportunities in Guttenberg, but they were not temptations. With Katherine he was having that rare thing, a love affair. An editor sleeping with his writer was not as bad as a psychoanalyst sleeping with his patient, or even a professor sleeping with an undergraduate, let alone a president with an intern; nevertheless, when he'd left his wife and moved in with Katherine, a couple of envious senior colleagues at Page and Turner had taken him aside to warn him against the explosive mixture of too many kinds of intimacy, and wheeled out stories of editors who had lost star writers, and novelists who had dried up or, worse, started to write mawkish and baggy prose.

Katherine was not a star yet but she was full of promise, and everyone at Page and Turner hoped and expected to see her latest novel, *Consequences*, on the Elysian Short List. There wasn't a line he hadn't pondered and polished. He had boldly changed the chapter order and meticulously tightened the plot. It had been a real collaboration. He had watched some of the sentences form on her computer screen while he kissed her neck and ran his hands over her body, not sure whether he preferred to distract or inspire her. They lay in bed at weekends, Katherine writing the next chapter while he edited the one before. Being so close to her writing made Alan realize that Katherine's enthralling sexuality was only part of a broader erotic relationship with experience. She wrote the sentences of someone who trails her fingers over the furniture she admires and inhales the scent of a melon before slicing it open, who touches what she can touch, but also expects the most abstruse ideas to turn into sensations as her imagination takes them in.

He had only just made the Elysian deadline, hanging on to the typescript until the last moment in case there was something still to be done; two sentences turned into one, one sentence broken into two, the substitution of a slightly resistant adjective to engender a moment's reflection, in short, the joys of editing, all carried out without forgetting the art that disguises art, giving the appearance of ease to the greatest difficulty and bringing clarity to tangled and obscure ideas. It had been a terrible wrench when he handed the typescript to his assistant to get it biked over to the Elysian people on that final afternoon, but he knew that the collaboration would continue. He would help Katherine to find exactly the right way to describe the novel in interviews and, if all went well, the right tone for her speech at the Elysian dinner.

As his taxi turned into Gloucester Terrace, Alan spotted Didier Leroux and Sam Black, both looking rather crumpled, as if they had been drinking all night and hadn't had time to go home and change. Sam was a novelist who Alan might one day tempt over to Page and Turner, if he could get him for a reasonable price. Didier, on the other hand, he dreaded seeing, not only because he was an ex-boyfriend of Katherine's who didn't seem to know when he was beaten, but also because he was always trying to get Alan to publish his books in England. His latest assault had been at a drinks party of Katherine's when he'd been trying to peddle his new book, *Qu'est-ce la Banalité?*.

'I'm sorry,' Alan said sensibly, 'but we can't publish a book in England called *What Is Banality?*.'

'Call it *The Anatomy of Banality*,' suggested Didier, following Alan into the kitchen. 'This will appeal to Anglo-Saxon materialism, and also the echo with *The Anatomy of Melancholy* signals that it's a serious work, no?'

'Of all things that don't need analysing,' Alan began, but Didier interrupted him straight away.

'Ah, *non*! We *think* we know what is banality, but in reality there is something very radical in the concept. When Chateaubriand says, "Everybody looks at what I look at, but nobody sees what I see", we have the tragic isolation of subjectivity, the heroic vision of Romanticism, and so on and so forth, but the radical moment of the banal is precisely the reversal of Chateaubriand. It announces: "Everybody looks at what I look at and everybody sees what I see". Epistemologically, this is the pure communism! Communism has not been realized in the state of China, or Russia, or Cuba, but in the state of Banality!'

As a man who had just come back from a conference in Europe, Alan was wholly committed to a borderless continent of high-speed trains and fluid exchanges of rich cultural traditions, but as he passed the pair he couldn't help wishing that Didier would go back to Paris where he belonged.

The conference had turned out to be a trade fair for digital gadgets and fatuous theories. His worst two hours were spent with an extremely pretty Korean-American girl, who gradually eroded the effect of her physical allure by trying to persuade Alan that the future of fiction lay with Alternate Narrative, an 'empowering and proactive' software that allowed the reader to choose alternate outcomes.

'It creates a participatory reality,' she explained, 'which is like a concrete experience of freedom in our lives and in our creative choices.' Two boxes appeared on the screen, one saying 'Kill' and the other, 'Don't Kill'.

'With Alternate Narrative the "language game" really *is* a language game,' she said with inexplicable mirth.

After a while she slowed down and entered into a more reflective relationship with her program.

'It *really* becomes a mirror for the user's psyche,' she said, staring at Alan as if they were trapped down a mine together. 'I mean if the reader chooses to kill a character, what does that say about the reader's own "character". In other words, what narrative are you in? What narrative are you in, *in your own life right now*?'

In the end, Alan had bought the program to save Monica from the humiliation of wasting so much emotional effort.

The taxi drew up outside Katherine's building and Alan, with a litre of airport vodka and an Alternate Narrative to sweeten his return, hurried inside.

Katherine was waiting for him in the hall. She was wearing her pale-green dressing gown with nothing underneath. They kissed and then he led her by the hand into the drawing room.

'How was your conference?' she asked.

'Completely banal,' he said, sinking into the big armchair. 'Talking of banality, I saw Didier in the street with Sam Black, just round the corner. I didn't know they were friends.'

'They've become friends through me,' she said, straddling the armchair, just as he'd imagined.

She was so perfect it took his breath away.

9

Penny had been asked by Malcolm to check out Tobias's favourite novel, *All the World's a Stage*. According to the blurb, it was 'an ambitious and original' novel, written by a young New Zealander from the point of view of William Shakespeare. It gave a 'richly textured portrait of Jacobean London', as well as taking the reader 'inside the mind of the greatest genius in all of human history'. Penny felt instinctively that this one would be a survivor. Choosing a New Zealander would be a salute to the Commonwealth and at the same time the theme was patriotic and educational. With the Long List being announced tomorrow, she plunged straight in. She couldn't wait.

'William!'
'Ben!'

'*Do you know Thomas Kyd and John Webster?*'

'*Lads,*' *said William, giving the men a friendly nod.*

Thomas returned his smile, but John continued to scowl out of the window, ignoring William.

'*John would as soon bastinado a man's shanks as shake his hand,*' *explained good Master Jonson.* '*He was not yet thirteen when he murdered the black-smith he was apprenticed to. News came in that day of great Marlowe's death and John was thrown into the blackest grief.* "*There's a great spirit gone,*" *quoth he.*

'"*Indeed the tears lie in an onion that should water that sorrow,*" *quoth the blacksmith, where-upon such a choleric humour came o'er John that he lifted the glowing poker from the coals of his master's furnace and plunged it into the wretched blacksmith's entrails. Never a man died with a more astonished expression on his face, unless it was King Edward, second of that name.*'

Before William could respond to this amazing tale of murder most foul, strange and unnatural, John rose up in his chair, in a state of great excitation, and pointed through the window.

'*All eyes! All eyes! My lord Essex comes hard upon us with a great retinue of men. How finely*

caparisoned they are, and point device in their accou-
trement.'

'Oh happy horse that bears the weight of Essex,'
said William, straining out of the casement to catch
a glimpse.

'See how his mount's proud impatient hoof doth
ring fire from the cobblestones!' said old Thomas
Kyd. 'How like a god is he in countenance, in bear-
ing how like a king.'

William sank back down next to Master Ben
despondently.

'My pleasure lies in Essex,' he sighed, 'but I wait in
vain for any sign, or any summons. I am a mere slave
that tends upon the hours and times of his desire.'

'Come, William,' said Ben, slapping him on the
shoulder, 'enough of that. Let us have one more
gaudy night and mock the midnight bell. I have sold
my latest play to this innkeeper for five shillings of
sack. He understands not a word of it, poor fool, but
hopes to sell it for a profit to the Chancellor's Men.'

'Would I had a play to sell,' said William, 'and
we would have roasted capons withal, but I only
started one this morning and shall not finish it till
the morrow.'

'What is its argument?' asked Ben.

'Why, 'tis a Roman play,' said William. 'It tells the tale of Anthony and how one of the three pillars of this world was made into a strumpet's fool.'

Penny couldn't help admiring the way it made you feel you were really in a tavern with William Shakespeare and his pals. That was the wonderful thing about historical novels, one met so many famous people. It was like reading a very old copy of *Hello!* magazine. She read on eagerly.

'Speaking of strumpets,' said Thomas, 'is that not Mistress Lucretia that comes hard upon us?'

'Ah,' said William, 'now let us speak of Africa and golden joys. She comes so perfumed that the winds are love-sick that follow her.'

The fair Lucretia hoisted up her skirts, the better to straddle William's legs.

'Fye, William,' she said, clicking his golden earring against her teeth, 'where is that sonnet you promised me?'

'Why, 'tis in my codpiece,' said William, 'for a man is a fool who keeps not a poem in his codpiece, and a codpiece that hath no poem in it is indeed a foolish codpiece.'

'It is a naughty codpiece,' said John, 'for it hath naught in it.'

'Ho-ho,' said goodly Master Jonson, draining his tankard of sack, 'a battle of wits!'

'With this naught,' said William, clasping Lucretia by the waist and pulling her towards him, 'I shall make a copy of thy fair face; I shall so plough thy field with this nothing that it will yield thee a crop of Lucretias. With this round O I shall make thy belly round, and by my death,' he added, shuddering and sinking backwards in his chair, 'I shall make thee immortal.'

'Fye, Will,' said Lucretia, arching backwards and pulling William towards her, 'keep thy wit for thy plays, for wit is a poor actor that comes on and plays his part and leaves the stage and is heard no more, but the part I would have you play hath more will in it than wit.'

Penny was definitely going to give *All the World's a Stage* the thumbs up. It was chock-a-block with colourful characters and period detail, just like her other favourite, *The Enigma Conundrum*, a real page-turner about the 'Enigma' code-breaking operation at Bletchley Park during the Second World War, which included a marvellous portrait of the brilliant, but alas gay, Alan Turing, the Cambridge mathematician who had done the thinking behind the computer. There was also a portrait of the unsung hero who had built Colossus, the first actual computer, right here in Britain. After the War, this ordinary postal worker had simply got on his bike and gone back to repairing people's telephones. No commercial fortune, or Nobel Prize, or knighthood for him, just the quiet pride of knowing that he had served his country in its hour of need. Marvellous, inspirational stuff, so unlike today's attention-seeking, get-rich-quick culture, in which people did things they were completely unqualified for just to get their name in the papers. The novel's portrait of Churchill was utterly convincing – you could almost smell the cigar smoke and the brandy on his breath!

Apart from anything else, one actually learned something from such a well-researched book, which was more than could be said of the neurotic musings of a lot of writers stuck at home, reading, writing and thinking about literature. Why didn't they get out and do something for a change? Work in public service, or in a factory, or teach in a school; get out of their narrow little worlds and meet some real people; anything rather than sit at home all day writing.

It was a strange experience for Penny to be seeing Jo Cross in the flesh. Although she rather avoided Jo's op-ed pieces, sounding off on every subject from Abortion to Zimbabwe, Penny was a huge fan of *The Home Front*, Jo's weekly column complaining about her husband and children. Jo was a strong advocate of a novel called *The Palace Cookbook*, published by an Indian firm with only one other book on its list. That was enough to get Jo to take up the cudgels on its behalf, sticking up for the underdog. She appeared to have made a deal with Malcolm, winning his support for *The Palace Cookbook* in exchange for supporting *wot u starin at*. Jo was also keen on a book called *A Year in the Wild*, a Canadian novel about a disillusioned hedge-fund manager who leaves his power-crazed life on Wall Street in order to build a log cabin in the wilderness of British Columbia. Jo said that with the financial meltdown and the state of the environment, it was one of the novels that had come top in her 'relevance' test.

As well as *wot u starin at*, Malcolm had chosen *The Bruce*, an action-packed novel that really brought Scottish history alive, and *The Greasy Pole*, the story of a working-class lad from the Highlands who goes into politics and, without giving the plot away, ends up becoming Prime Minister of Britain, which was a remarkable achievement.

The only member of the committee Penny really found it hard to take was Vanessa Shaw. She was so frightfully intellectual, but not in fact, in Penny's opinion, really that clever. She was mad about a novel called *The Frozen Torrent*, which Penny had been unable to make any headway with. The whole thing was, according to Vanessa, 'built and unbuilt' on systematic self-contradiction, just as life was built on the contradiction of death (ugh!). Not only did the text (as if it had just popped up on her mobile phone!) show a deep reading of Beckett, Blanchot, and Bataille (whoever the last two were), but also brought to this 'self-corroding sensibility' (good God!), the richness of a profound and original psychological novel.

In other words, the author had stolen all his ideas and didn't just contradict himself by mistake (which, let's face it, happens to all of us, now and again) but actually *set out* to contradict himself! It made her blood boil to think that this charlatan, with his second-hand ideas and phrases, and his absurd habit of self-contradiction, was going to get his wretched novel on to the Long List.

Penny glanced at her watch. She'd better get a move on. It was no use dawdling at home day-dreaming about past meetings when she was due at the most important meeting yet: the one that would finalize the Long List and take the prize into a whole new phase.

10

Now that it was his turn to sit hunched in her arm-chair, his collarless shirt bulging and contracting with the grief that shuddered through his body, Katherine realized how little she knew Sonny. When she let him in to her flat he had barely greeted her before casting himself down and beginning to sob.

'What's wrong?' she asked.

'What's wrong?' said Sonny. 'I've been robbed of this year's Elysian Prize.'

'I didn't even know that you'd written a novel,' said Katherine.

'I've written an enduring work of art,' said Sonny, 'and they haven't even put me on their Long List!'

'*Consequences* isn't on the Long List either, thanks to my idiotic publisher,' said Katherine. 'He gave my novel to his assistant to send round on the day of the deadline and she sent your aunt's cookbook instead. Any other committee would have realized that there'd been a fuck-up and sent the cookbook back.'

'I'm sure you deserved to be on the Long List,' said Sonny. 'But I deserved to win!'

'Well, in that case,' said Katherine, 'I can't wait to read this masterpiece of yours.'

'There's a signed copy at Heywood Hill,' said Sonny. 'Don't tell the book fellow you're a friend of mine.'

'That'll be easy enough,' said Katherine. 'The only question is whether to camp overnight on the pavement outside.'

'I hope you're not being sarcastic with me,' said Sonny, brought upright by pique. 'My nerves really can't take it.'

'I'm sorry,' said Katherine, 'but I'm disappointed as well.'

'That's why we should form an alliance,' said Sonny.

'What for? Being disappointed?'

'For revenge, of course,' said Sonny. 'In a more enlightened age, the judges would have been dragged into a public square and horsewhipped.' His body relaxed for a moment under the softening influence of nostalgia. 'The furious multitude,' he went on, his hands spreading artistically as he imagined the scene, 'would have torn them limb from limb to punish them for insulting their betters! But in these degenerate times, I suppose we'll have to make do with a hired assassin. Do you know such a person? I tried to get a man sent over from Delhi, but they wouldn't give him a visa. Red tape!'

'You can't be serious,' said Katherine.

'Very well,' said Sonny, getting up with restored vigour and stepping back into his slippers. 'I see that you have no pride in yourself, but I am not, nor shall I ever be, in that pitiful condition! We shall see which one of us is truly serious about literature!'

Katherine waited tensely until she heard the front door close. She could imagine a time when she would have burst out laughing at the absurdity of Sonny's conversation and the relief of his departure, but she had been too angry in the last few days to laugh at anything.

She felt isolated, partly because she had turned her phone off, driven mad by constant calls from Alan, pleading to be taken back. The first day after she threw him out, he rang to say that he had sacked his assistant, and that she had left in tears.

'If you were right to sack her, I was right to sack you,' she answered coldly.

'I'll take her back if you'll take me back,' he said.

'Rivers don't flow upstream,' said Katherine.

'But I love you . . .'

She hung up before he could finish his unpromising sentence. Every few hours her inbox silted up with emails that she deleted without reading. Katherine had become disciplined about ending an affair; it was an indispensable skill for someone who had averaged twenty lovers a year since she was sixteen. Besides, Alan suddenly seemed so irrelevant, now that *Consequences* was no longer in the running for the Elysian. She had felt the same way about her English tutor at Cambridge after getting a First. He had been astonished, but to her it was the most natural thing in the world: why would anybody sleep with a don after leaving university? It was nothing to do with being mercenary, but it had everything to do with being impulsive. She slept with the man of the moment. The moment might be the way a man held his glass, or it might be more practical, like a don at university, but neither kind of moment could last, and when it ended there was nothing left. She knew that she would feel frightened and empty if she ever stopped, and so there was always someone to fall back on, or move on to.

Things were perilously close to empty right now. She had lost Sam the same day she lost Alan. *The Frozen Torrent* was on the Long List and she didn't feel like being patronized in bed. Sam didn't yet know about her decision, if decision was the right word for that snap in her psyche. As a result, in this disastrous week, only Didier was left and she was in no condition to organize anything else; she didn't want pity, or even sympathy, she wanted infatuation.

Katherine turned on her phone and it rang immediately.

'Oh, fuck off,' she said, looking at Alan's name on the screen. She ignored Alan and rang Didier.

'Can you come round?'

'When?'

'Straight away. It's just you.'

'*A bas le triangle! Vive le couple!*' said Didier. 'No Sam? No Alan?'

'I'm down to just you,' said Katherine.

'Down is good,' said Didier, 'it reduces the vertigo.'

'It is the vertigo,' said Katherine.

'Not once you've landed.'

'Well, let's land.'

'Okay, I abandon this wonderful sentence I am writing: "we think we are free because we lack the language to describe our unfreedom" . . .'

'Please,' said Katherine.

'Okay, *j'arrive*.'

11

'What is the purpose of art?' Sam felt doomed as he wrote the question. What did he really think?

'To arrest our attention in the midst of distraction.' Could he say that?

'Its uselessness is its supreme value. Money only has value because it can be exchanged for something else, art only has value because it can't.'

Try telling that to a Rembrandt owner, who's just exchanged a 'useless' self-portrait for twenty-seven million pounds, thought Sam, or for that matter to someone whose loneliness has been abolished by the perfect reflection of her mood or predicament in the sentence she has just read.

'To arrest our attention in the midst of distraction', or 'to distract our attention in the midst of fixation'. He could imagine approaching that point from the opposite angle. The whole thing was a nightmare. If he didn't pull himself together, he would have to come up with a Theory of Beauty.

'The purpose of style,' Sam began, 'is to generate interest', he concluded timidly.

What was interest? Talk about begging the question.

He marvelled at the speed with which elation had turned into anxiety. Ever since he had found that *The Frozen Torrent* was on the Long List, he had been torn between a superstitious need to avoid anticipating any further success, and a neurotic need to plan, in case further success came his way. What if he had to make a speech, the speech, in fact, of an Elysian winner? He didn't want to think about it, in case the gods punished him for expecting things to go well, but he must think about it, so as to pacify his fear of success.

One thing was clear; he was going to have to drop the topic of art. In England, art was much less likely to be mentioned in polite society than sexual perversions or methods of torture; the word 'elitist' could be spat out with the same confident contempt as 'coward' at a court martial. It seemed as if a prejudice could not be banished without driving some other topic, once freely discussed, or even admired, into a shameful exile. Perhaps in future generations a law would be passed allowing consenting adults to practise art openly; an Intellect Relations Board might be set up to encourage tolerance towards people who, through no fault of their own, were interested in ideas. Meanwhile, it was just as well to keep quiet and play the fool.

Whatever its contents, Sam preferred to speculate about a speech he would probably never have to make than to contemplate the agony of Katherine's defection. When *The Frozen Torrent* appeared on the Long List, and *Consequences* did not, she had broken contact with him. Was it envy or disappointment? Was she ill, or was she dead? She ignored as many messages as he dared to send. He hoped feverishly that the equation of literary success and erotic failure was reversible, and that she would take him back if his novel didn't make the Short List, but a quieter, saner voice told him that he would just end up with both kinds of failures at once.

In the end he was driven to ring Didier for news.

'This imbecile she used to live with,' Didier explained, 'sent a cookbook to the judges instead of her novel.'

'What?' said Sam, who thought he must have mis-heard.

'No, no, it gets better,' said Didier. 'They put the cookbook on the Long List. This is no joke. We are entering the Dark Ages, my friend, but this time there will be lots of neon, and screen savers, and street lighting. This is the Dark Ages with light pollution: with the pollution of the Enlightenment! The pigs are wandering among the temple ruins; women are being raped on the steps of the forgotten Senate; there are only two or three monks who can still read in the whole of Europe; all of that, naturally, but this time it's going to be on TV! This time it's going to be famous! It's going to give interviews: "It's not so easy being the Dark Ages, there are many problems: I think I need some therapy, et cetera." You get the picture? Only Lacan can do justice to this over-illuminated Dark Age, because only he has the obscurity to survive!'

'Did you say, "used to live"?' asked Sam tenaciously. 'Do you mean Alan Oaks doesn't live with her any more?'

'Evidently, she has thrown him out,' Didier confirmed.

'So, are you still seeing her?'

'She doesn't want to see anybody,' said Didier, 'but we are old friends, and so she allows me to bring her some food, some wine: the bare necessities.'

'I see,' said Sam.

'She knows she is living at the end of civilization,' said Didier, 'because I am the one who told her!' He burst out laughing. 'Everybody thinks they understand the joke of reality TV, but the real joke is that there is no other reality! There can be no civilization because we are living in the desert of the Real. All our experience has been mediated by a system whose tyranny is precisely that no one controls it. Its tyranny is the absence of the tyrant! We have made a catastrophic progress since Bentham's Panoptic prison: we no longer need the supervision of The Other, we are prisoners of our own gaze! When we think we are having an original thought, we are in fact remembering an episode from the soap opera of global capitalism. Our most private fantasies have already been marketed . . .'

'Yes, well, never mind the end of civilization,' Sam interrupted him, 'what about the end of my relationship with Katherine?'

'That is a personal matter,' said Didier. 'Ask me about the nature of the human condition, or the limits of language, but you and Katherine, this fragile human relationship, it's too complex.' Didier allowed himself a little giggle at the idea that there was a subject too complex for his critical capacities. 'But what is love, really?' he went on. 'When we speak of the game we call "love", what . . .'

Sam said goodbye hastily, before hearing Didier's views on this important topic. He needed to take in all this news. He was delighted that Katherine was no longer living with Alan, but annoyed that Didier was still sleeping with her. On the other hand, she couldn't be expected to put up with his preposterous theorizing for much longer. Sam realized that he would have to keep in touch with Didier in order to choose the right time to re-submit his application to Katherine. If she went off with some entirely new lover, his access to her would become even more tenuous.

He got up from his desk and collapsed, with a sigh, onto the sofa in the centre of his living room. In that moment of slight exaggeration, Didier's last question returned to him reproachfully, and he couldn't help wondering whether love could really consist of an unpleasant combination of obsession, self-pity, rivalry, lust and daydreaming. These characteristics didn't seem to distinguish it from the rest of life, except by their intensity. He was allowing Katherine to act on him like one of Didier's absent tyrants, rather than another suffering human being. He must pull himself together and make an effort to imagine what she was going through.

He sat upright and rested his eyes contemplatively on the empty fireplace. She must be feeling miserable about *Consequences*, after five years of work. It can't have been simple to throw Alan out, after he had left his wife for her. Sam's empathy ground into action, and as he imagined the details of Katherine's personality, it started to take on subtlety and depth. He gradually filtered out his private relationship with the emotions he imagined she was having. His whole state of mind became sharper and more generous. This still wasn't love, but it was an environment in which love could prosper, unlike the self-centred misery of the last few days. If only she were with him now and could see how much love he had to give, surely she would be asking for his forgiveness, as she unbuttoned his shirt, right here on the blue sofa.

Sam keeled over and sprawled among the cushions, groaning.

12

Although the hostile response to the Elysian Long List had exceeded his expectations, Malcolm still felt that a certain amount of media indignation was not only inevitable but desirable. It showed that his committee had the courage to choose fresh, original and exciting new voices and not just hand out free tickets to the darlings of the literary establishment. Vanessa Shaw was the exception, doing her best to promote the interests of the old guard. Although her three choices were now the favourites at Ladbrokes, Malcolm had no intention of being dictated to by writers, academics, publishers, readers, journalists, booksellers, literary critics or, least of all, betting shops. *The Greasy Pole* was languishing at 25–1, which was a gross distortion of its artistic value as well as its standing among members of the committee.

In politics he spoke in paragraphs he had been
using for decades, or deployed old arguments that
could effortlessly be adapted to modern occasions,
but at the announcement of the Long List, he suddenly had a feeling of being publicly exposed and
vulnerable in a way he hadn't experienced since the
first time he represented Aberdeen Grammar School
in a debating contest. He was supposed to be arguing in favour of Ian Smith's Unilateral Declaration
of Independence. He was told that by arguing for a
cause he vehemently opposed, he would hone his
pure debating skills. Instead, it left him feeling blank
and fraudulent, just as he had at the press conference.
The journalists asked questions about books he
hadn't read that were on the List, as well as about
books he hadn't read that weren't on the List. In the
end, which was not far from the beginning, he just
snapped.

'That's our List – like it or not.'

The press enjoyed pretending that the selection
process took place in an atmosphere of antagonism
and incompetence, whereas in fact the meetings had
been perfectly friendly so far, thanks partly to Penny's
obliging nature, to some skilful deal-making between
Jo and himself, and to Tobias's total absence. Vanessa's

pedantic championing of literary tradition and her undergraduate lectures on the art of the novel did no real harm, although she was going to be in for a rude awakening when it came to carrying her three candidates forward to the next stage. He would let her keep one, preferably *The Frozen Torrent*, whose author was the least well established.

Right from the start, Malcolm had laid down some ground rules with a speech he made about 'social responsibility'.

'We have eighty thousand pounds at our disposal, as well as the promise of several hundred thousand pounds which the winner can expect to earn over the next few years, and to me it's of paramount importance that the money goes to someone who really needs it.'

'It's lucky Proust or Nabokov aren't competing this year,' said Vanessa, 'or Henry James, or Tolstoy, or anyone who ever sold a novel because word got out that it was worth reading, like Dickens, or Thackeray, or . . .'

'All right, all right,' said Jo, 'we all know that you've read every book under the sun, but I think Malcolm has a very good point. If I had my way I would add, "no pseuds and no aristos".'

'Gosh,' said Vanessa, 'in the bad old days of hatred and prejudice, you might have said, "no yids, no niggers and no women", but thank God we live in a more enlightened age, and we've finally got the list right.'

'And no gays,' said Penny. 'I mean, in the bad old days,' she added hastily.

'We want to take the marginalized, and the politically repressed voices from the periphery,' said Malcolm, ignoring the spat between the ladies, 'from what we might call the Outer Hebrides of the literary scene, and bring them centre stage. Now, as we know, there are a lot of vested interests that have got used to the idea that the literary scene belongs to them, and when we reclaim it for the ordinary readers of this country, let's not pretend they're going to thank us for it.'

'Who's "they"?' said Vanessa. 'The readers?'

'The vested interests of course.'

'Oh, I see. It wasn't grammatically clear.'

'I think it was perfectly clear from the context,' said Malcolm, refusing to be provoked.

'The vested interests are certainly not going to thank us,' said Jo. 'And all I can say is that if they want a fight, we're ready for them.'

'They think it's some kind of scandal,' said Malcolm, 'if we don't agree with their judgements, but the real scandal is that they're trying to dictate to the duly appointed Elysian Prize committee.'

'Before we all stand up and sing "The Internationale",' said Vanessa, 'do you think we could take a glance at what we've been "duly appointed" to do?'

And then she launched into one of her patronizing tutorials on the true nature of literature.

The only committee member with whom Malcolm was on absolutely perfect terms was Tobias Benedict, whose stream of charming postcards, apologizing for his unavoidable absence, arrived every few days from Leeds and Sheffield, Manchester and Brighton, as he toured the country playing Estragon in a hip-hop adaptation of *Waiting for Godot*.

For Malcolm, Tobias was the key to a majority vote. It was increasingly clear that Vanessa was Malcolm's opponent and although he had formed a working coalition with Jo, she was far too fond of having her own way for their alliance to hold in the closing phases of the competition. Penny Feathers, on the other hand, was all eagerness and obedience and had a natural inclination to follow authority. As long as she stayed on side, it all depended on Tobias.

Malcolm had given him the impression that he was Tobias's only friend on the committee and that he had carefully steered *All the World's a Stage* onto the Long List, out of respect for his views and admiration for an 'astonishing achievement'. Tobias had written back saying that he found *wot u starin at* 'terrifyingly vivid' and that it made 'a welcome change from a novel about a failing marriage in Hampstead – not that I seem to have ever read one, but you know what I mean!' Meanwhile, Malcolm was inviting Penny to dinner at the House of Commons at least once a fortnight, a brush with the corridors of power that she clearly valued. In other words, Malcolm was taking care of what really mattered: running the committee.

13

Nothing was quite so complicated, Sonny decided, as trying to find exactly the right costume for an assassination. One could neither delegate, nor consult, nor show off one's sartorial authority.

'Only a flunky would wear that sort of costume to a murder,' was exactly the sort of remark he had been forced to suppress again and again, as he trailed despondently past rows of suits made from materials he could scarcely bear to look at, let alone touch.

He had started out thinking that he would go with the timeless classicism of black: black balaclava, black polo-neck sweater, black trousers, black shoes with (alas the day) rubber soles, and some sort of short black jacket, possibly (or rather, impossibly!) with a zip. When the Harrods mirror revealed a figure who could easily have been mistaken for a bouncer on the door of a low dive in the East End, Sonny rebelled against the dreary modern uniform he had been assembling, and stormed back to his waiting car. Only the balaclava and the polo neck survived, while the rest of his repulsively slippery shopping bags were deposited by his driver into the arms of a far from grateful gypsy woman who beat on the window of the Bentley demanding cash, while her daughter, wearing an identical headscarf, pointed vigorously at her mouth, as if trying to make herself sick. It astonished Sonny to reflect that in India a beggar would be prepared to drag his trolley along half a mile of filthy ground with only the use of his chin, praising all the generations of his benefactor's family if a small coin was tossed in his direction, whereas here, against the backdrop of this monumental department store, its rusty facade pimpled with wasteful light bulbs, a thousand pounds of untouched Italian menswear elicited only fury and resentment!

With the impatience of a man who is being rushed by ambulance to an accident and emergency ward, Sonny ordered his driver to take him to Savile Row. He was guided by a new vision of how to remain in black without taking on the appearance of a proletarian thug: a dinner jacket. Why had he not thought of it before?

By noon he was in a soothingly large, panelled changing room, surrounded by framed bills made out to royal personages and legendary actors, as well as brief letters of condescending satisfaction signed by similar persons. He immediately felt at home. As luck would have it, a proper bespoke dinner jacket, of slimming double-breasted cut, made for a mysterious customer, perhaps dead or ruined, who had never bothered to pick it up, had been languishing in a cupboard reserved for that purgatorial category of half paid but uncollected garments, and was now being brought to him by an assiduous tailor in whose opinion it would suit Sonny very well.

The tailor's eye had not deceived him. Sonny gazed in awe at the perfection of the fit. The trousers were six inches too long, but that was the most trifling of alterations. In his excitement, he telephoned his driver and asked him to bring the sweater and the balaclava, specifying that they should be taken out of their plastic bags. Once they arrived, he wriggled into the polo-neck sweater, and after replacing the jacket and doing up its inner and outer buttons, pulled the balaclava over his head. He then turned towards the slightly tilted full-length mirror and looked with admiration, and a touch of foreboding, at the elegant and menacing figure staring back at him. He extended his right arm, clasping it with his left hand to support the weight of an imaginary pistol, and spinning around as best he could in such a long pair of trousers, fired round after round with deadly accuracy into the chests and foreheads of the five Elysian Prize judges.

With the balaclava covering his ears and his mind filled with scenes of daring and stylish revenge, Sonny didn't notice the tailor until he caught sight of him standing respectfully at the back of the changing room. What had he seen? Could Sonny count on his silence?

'I did knock, sir . . .' the tailor began.

'No, no,' said Sonny, removing his balaclava and tossing it onto a nearby chair, 'come in. I, er,' he struggled for an explanation, 'sometimes like to ski in just such a costume.'

'I imagine there's a good deal of formal wear at some of the better resorts,' said the tailor.

'Absolutely!' said Sonny, regaining his momentum. 'One often, you know, *schusses* to a big party already changed for dinner!'

'Of course, sir,' said the tailor, turning Sonny gently towards the mirror and running his hands appreciatively down the sides of the dinner jacket. 'Just as I thought, sir, it might have been made for you.'

Sonny was so elated by his new purchase that he decided to walk the length of Savile Row, telling the driver to wait for him on the far corner. He strolled down the street, glancing into the broad windows of renowned tailors, each with its trio of headless mannequins, displaying a variety of such alluring costumes that by the time he reached Burlington Gardens, Sonny found his imagination was already drifting towards an alternative costume. Why not take a week's deer stalking in Scotland? On the day ordained for his revenge, he would have a plane waiting to take him to Inverness. Under the circumstances it would be eminently plausible for him to be wearing a pale green tweed such as he'd seen a few windows down, with a faint sky blue over-check, a cream silk shirt with a simple dark green or golden brown knitted tie. If the police questioned him about wearing these emphatically country clothes in the middle of Mayfair, he need only mention the shooting lodge he had taken in the Highlands and show them evidence of his imminent plane flight, and their suspicions would dissolve. They wouldn't bother to open the boot of his car, and if they did, what could be more natural than to find a deer-stalking rifle lying innocently in its case?

A gun! Of course, he needed a gun! Sonny pressed a steadying hand on the roof of his car. He felt like a traveller who arrives at the check-in desk, only to realize that he has left his passport on the dressing table at home. How could he have forgotten? Back in Badanpur he had a splendid hunting rifle: the very weapon with which his grandfather had shot over two hundred tigers. One couldn't shoot two hundred tigers nowadays without buying them first from several city zoos. There wouldn't be much sport in releasing a bewildered urban tiger into the wild and magnificent, if somewhat shrunken, forests of Badanpur. The wretched tiger would probably be mobbed by gazelles, like an eligible schoolboy surrounded by insatiable women at his first big dance!

The red tape involved in trying to get his grandfather's rifle sent over from India would no doubt outweigh the atavistic pleasure and lyrical beauty of using it to destroy his detractors. Sonny got into his car and ordered the driver to return him to the hotel.

He was soon beached on a pink sofa in the Arnold Bennett suite, among the wreckage of a Full English tea. Suddenly feeling the melancholy of those empty plates, he pinched the last few strands of watercress and placed them listlessly in his mouth. Planning a murder was such a lonely business and such a strain on the nerves.

The phone rang, lifting him out of his torpor. For a moment he wondered if he could face answering it, but the prospect of alleviating his loneliness got the better of him.

'Auntie!'

'Sonny, my dear, how are you?' said Auntie, without pausing for an answer. 'I'm planning a little trip to London. There's been such a hullabaloo about *Palace*, I thought I should come over in person. Apparently, I've written a great novel, which I suppose is true, but really I set out to write a cookery book. It's too amusing, when I think of all the people who are struggling to write a great novel, that I've done it without even noticing.'

'Quite,' said Sonny drily. 'Will you be bringing Mansur with you?' he asked, trying not to sound as inspired as he felt.

'Why would I want that brute to come to London with me?

'Well,' said Sonny, improvising wildly, 'my back has completely *gone*, I mean *completely*, and I need someone to carry me around.'

'Can't Claridge's help?' said Auntie irritably.

'Well, you know how it is in the West,' said Sonny, 'everyone is so spoilt; they've lost any idea of service or gratitude. Only this morning a beggar I'd been showering with gifts chased me down the street! Instead of thanking me, she completely lost her temper! I need someone who will sleep on the floor at the foot of my bed, without complaining. I'll take care of his fare, of course.'

'Very well,' said Auntie with a click of her tongue.

When the conversation was over, Sonny clapped his hands with delight. He had always coveted Mansur, Auntie's ferocious nightwatchman. He sometimes thought that Mansur took more pride in the Badanpur clan than Sonny himself, if such a thing were possible. The man was a human mountain. There would be no need to provide him with a firearm; he could tear apart the impudent judges with his bare hands.

Sonny felt himself irradiated by a divine presence.

He saw now that all the trials of the day had been Krishna's way of protecting him from the strain of personally dispatching Malcolm Craig, MP. His ancestor Krishna had sent him Mansur. Truly, the gods were on his side.

14

The only luxury left to Alan was that brief passage before he was fully awake, before the hazy disorientation that surrounded his drugged sleep was replaced by the solid horror of his circumstances. The woman he loved, the woman he had left his wife for, had thrown him out. His pleas to be taken back by Katherine had been utterly ignored, and his humiliating but pragmatic request to be taken back by Marilyn had been angrily rejected.

He moved into a hotel near his office in Pimlico. It was cheap in every respect, except for the cost of spending a night there. When he returned from work each evening, he pressed the trembling orange light switch in his corridor, buying a few fluorescent seconds to fit the key into his bedroom door. A man at the peak of his training might have opened the door in time, but for the forlorn and drunken Alan it was out of the question. After feeling around the keyhole in the dark, stabbing his finger a couple of times, and finally unlocking the door, he stumbled into a room that made him long to go out again. The dingy net curtains were disturbed by a draught from the ill-fitting window; the mustard yellow bedspread was made of a synthetic fabric that must have originally been designed for experiments in static electricity; and on a small stained tray, next to sachets of instant coffee that had withstood generations of indifference, there were three little plastic pots of milk whose claims to long life made his own seem all the more tenuous.

The hotel's proximity to his office lost its charm once the Russian proprietor of Page and Turner sacked Alan for his failure to submit *Consequences* to the Elysian committee, and for Katherine's subsequent threats of defection. It had long been rumoured that Yuri (as everyone chose to call him, preferring not to embark on the polysyllabic slalom course of his surname) had been drawn to the august and bankrupt firm of Page and Turner by his fascination with Katherine Burns rather than his passion for English letters. Either way, he had acquired it, and its debts, for one pound. The world was evenly and quite heatedly divided over the question of whether Yuri and Katherine had slept together. Alan had the misfortune of knowing the truth. Katherine had granted Yuri a few nights and then manufactured a stricken conscience over going to bed with a married man. Mrs Yuri was known to be the merciless partner, who took care of the brutalities of her husband's business, freeing him to be relatively gallant and agreeable. During the breakup of their brief affair, Katherine had known that Yuri would not make any reckless gestures, or even mendacious claims about leaving his wife. Instead, he softened Katherine with a persistent rain of opera tickets and orchids, as well as a gigantic advance they both knew she would never earn out.

Alan realized that he had really been fired for making Yuri jealous. To be punished for his intimacy with Katherine just as she ceased to acknowledge his existence deepened his sense of injustice. Not only had the incompetence over the typescript not been his, the competitiveness with Yuri had not been his, and now the intimacy with Katherine was not his either. Yuri, on the other hand, could count on Katherine's meticulous thank-you notes and prompt replies, and the fact that she would eventually be persuaded to stay at Page and Turner by another preposterous advance for a still more distant book.

Without his salary, Alan could no longer afford his room in the Mount Royal Hotel. He had guiltily handed over his savings to his abandoned wife, but he still had enough money in his current account and a good enough credit record, he hoped, to rent a room somewhere in outer London. He told the hotel that he was leaving, but to his surprise, on the morning of his departure he was suddenly overcome with lethargy. He wanted to be practical, to search for a room to rent, but somehow everything was too much, and he sprawled on the bed all morning, dressed but unable to leave. He tried to rationalize the feeling as a need for the hotel's central location, the convenience of a single bill compared with a plethora of household bills, broken boilers and toasted toasters in a rented room, but the truth was that he felt terribly tired. Why not stay a few more days? He had three credit cards, after all, with a combined overdraft capacity of fifteen thousand pounds. Perhaps, in the end, the best thing to do was to stare at the ceiling of his bedroom and sleep as much as possible. If only he could get to sleep, he would sleep for a thousand years.

At first Alan resisted the cliché of an unshaven depressive, but then, reflecting bitterly that he was no longer being paid to uproot cliché, he abandoned shaving with a certain vicious pleasure. The initial energy of his self-neglect depended on a barely acknowledged theatricality: he expected someone to notice, to be shocked, to offer to wash his clothes or run him a bath, but after a week or two his expanding sense of loneliness vaporized these imaginary friends. His actions were no longer gestures, and without the incentive to communicate, they were engulfed by his all-consuming fatigue. As he lay on his bed, the basin seemed so far away that the idea of brushing his teeth made him think of Livingstone's search for the source of the Nile. He imagined the terrible mountain ranges of his yellow bedspread; native bearers falling off the cliff of his mattress with piercing cries; the delirium of a tropical fever; his excruciating boots slippery with blood; the forbidding overhang of smooth white porcelain in the final ascent. He was so small that he might disappear at any moment, so little able to move that the inertia might spread to his heart and stop it beating.

There was a sheer fall, not at the end of things where it belonged, at the end of thought, or language, or at both ends of the visible spectrum, like horizons to our cognitive capacities, elegant, expected, almost reassuring; there was a sheer fall in between the things he used to take for granted, between instinct and desire, between desire and will, between will and action, between this and that, between one thing and another; gaps, crevasses, open wounds, broken circuits. How could he not have noticed before? What had he been doing all his life? Zipping along as if the ground were not groundless. He was like a toddler who has just been taught the word for something ubiquitous, and sits in his chair on the motorway, saying 'car' every time there happens to be one in view.

After two weeks the hotel management insisted that he let the maid in to clean the room. Alan, who had not eaten for several days, found that his aversion to staying in the room with the maid outweighed his aversion to moving at all, and so he went out, bearded, dishevelled, unwashed, and muttering his new word, 'Gap . . . gap . . . gap,' as he hurried hungrily down the street, close to the railings, avoiding the cracks in the paving stones.

15

The text that was dominating Vanessa's thoughts, as she sat at home, looking out at the bird feeder hanging from the apple tree in her back garden, was not one of the Elysian Prize submissions, nor indeed was it the PhD thesis she was supervising, in which the semi-colon had just arrived obscurely from Italy and was being disseminated into English literature by the erudite Ben Jonson; the text she couldn't get off her mind was written by her daughter.

In a perversion of filial piety, Poppy had asked Vanessa to use her critical skills to improve the little manifesto she was writing for a 'pro-ana' website, extolling the hidden ecstasies of her suicidal eating disorder. Vanessa felt that her relationship with her daughter had now gone irretrievably through the looking glass – the very same looking glass in which

Poppy saw her skeletal and hirsute body as a repel-
lent mass of white flab. The piece was hand-written,
with no corrections, in a pink notebook, with a brass
clasp holding its covers together. It rested on the
small round table next to Vanessa, looking more like
the diary of a fourteen-year-old girl than the exercise
book of a grown woman. Vanessa didn't need to
read it again, couldn't face reading it again. It was a
defiant prose poem on the subject of emaciation and
the beatitude of extreme hunger, the 'breakthrough'
when the 'gherlin gremlin' (gherlin, it turned out, was
the hormone for hunger) turned into 'the radiance',
the single-pointedness, the febrile quickness, 'the
humming wire'. Ranged against these incisive mental
joys was the cunning enemy and intolerable tempta-
tion of food, as if every scrap were as tragic as Eve's
first bite of the forbidden fruit – a fall, a rush of
shame, an exile from the luminous sphere of control
and self-sufficiency; a self-sufficiency that would one
day go beyond the rejection of food and liquid, and
perfect itself by discarding air as well.

If only this constriction in her chest and throat
could be expressed in tears, but Vanessa had never
found it easy to cry and she knew that there was little
point in looking for relief in that direction. She heard

the front door open and close. It was Tom, who was at home revising, coming back from a 'walk'. There was no point in greeting him, or offering him anything. He always returned from his walks reeking of grass and bolted back to his bedroom as soon as he came in. The boy in the coma from the ayahuasca weekend had died, but far from making Tom wake up from his stoned life, it seemed to have become the pretext for smoking elegiac joints with mutual acquaintances. He had asked Vanessa to recommend a poem he could read at 'a kind of wake thing' they had organized.

'I didn't really know him,' Tom told her. 'But it was really bad luck. It must have been some sort of allergic reaction – I mean everyone else had an amazing time.'

'You can't imagine how happy it makes me to hear that,' said Vanessa, with what she assumed was devastating sarcasm.

'Yeah,' said Tom with a survivor's laugh. 'I could have done without the snakes. I mean there were snakes *everywhere*, coming out of the walls, out of the eye of the little cockerel in the cornflakes package, pretty weird stuff, but then they kind of died away and it was all about *light*, about everything being basically *light*.'

She was reluctantly flattered that he chose to share his hallucinations with her, but only in the context of being appalled that he was cultivating hallucinations in the run-up to his A-levels. She felt parentally paralysed; anything Tom did could be cast in a recreational or exploratory light compared to his sister's illness. Besides, hadn't she and Stephen taught him that the best way to secure their attention was to be in trouble?

They were all sticks in the whirlpool of Poppy's ferocious will, the weaker she became physically, the stronger her psychological pull. A principled hunger strike, like Gandhi's, which was aimed at achieving something in the outside world, looked very impure and compromised compared to a hunger strike whose sole object was to stop eating: this was the white on white of the hunger strike, the moment when it became abstract and transcended the clumsy literalness of merely representing one thing or another.

She felt a violent desire to tear the bird feeder off its branch, and then she realized she was thinking of King Lear after Cordelia's death. Why should a bird have life when Poppy . . .

And then she found herself wondering why any book should win this fucking prize she had become involved with unless it had a chance of doing what had just happened: coming back to a person when she wanted to cry but couldn't, or wanted to think but couldn't think clearly, or wanted to laugh but saw no reason to.

16

'The rank sweat of an enseamed bed', thought
Katherine, sensing the dampness of the sheets as she
reached for the clock on the bedside table. It had
been flattened by Didier when he knocked over the
lamp and sent it to the floor with a muffled clatter
that echoed her own scattered climax better than the
groans of ecstasy, whimpers of disbelief, and an in-
congruous gasp of '*Oh, la vache!*' emanating from
the orgasmic Theorist.

It was eleven thirty-four on the morning of
another formless day, without professional obligations, or medical appointments, or even social
engagements, becalmed in a vast Pacific of self-
employment. Didier was next door, oppressing her
with his riotous creativity, tossing off another chapter on some neglected paradox, or hidden 'scandal'

of semiotics. She could hear the pensive mumblings and triumphant yelps that accompanied his energetic style of writing and she found them, in their way, even more annoying than his cries of sexual pleasure.

Katherine was suffering from a familiar seducer's gloom. Just as a 'good shot' might kill two hundred partridges over a weekend without being expected to eat them all for dinner on Sunday night, a woman with Katherine's genius for engendering desire and devotion couldn't be expected to deal with all of its consequences. She lived for the moment of submission, and although it lasted a little longer than the moment when a bird jerks its head backwards and starts to plummet through the air, she sometimes wished that Yuri and Alan and Sam and Didier, and all the others, could be lined up on the ground at the end of the year and become, like Don Giovanni's conquests, purely numerical. *Mille e tre! Mille e tre! Mille e tre!*

Where was her staying power? Where was the patience that might turn her gift for sudden intimacy into lasting love? She felt a spasm of loneliness, but not of the kind that could be cured by running to Didier; the only cure was to run away from him into the shallows of a new affair. She was reminded of the beach her family used to go to in Devon when she was a child, sloping gently into the sea and then, under the swell of the milky brown water, suddenly dropping away. She used to panic when she had been swimming too long, needing each wave to take her back to the slope, where her stretched foot could feel the gritty sand against her skin.

When she was fourteen she had watched her father die of a bee sting nobody knew he was allergic to. His face swelling and his throat swelling, while she sat with him beside the pool of their rented holiday house in Spain, his windpipe closing and letting in less and less air, while her mother, who never fully understood, because she didn't have to watch it happening, rushed off to the local pharmacy and came back too late.

A thousand hours of psychotherapy had done their familiar work, making an intellectually obvious truth into a deeply felt one. She knew that her anxiety about being abandoned made her compulsively abandon anyone who got close to her. Her father's death had ensured that she would never put herself in a position to receive another blow of that sort – or get out of the position of expecting one. What the psychotherapy had to wait for life to provide was this moment of ripeness and crisis. Nothing so stubborn could change until it became more painful to avoid than to confront. That crisis had come, but she still had no idea what action to take.

There was a professional (but certainly not romantic) option in the form of John Elton, the American literary agent, who had left a message inviting her to lunch.

She had first met John Elton in his New York agency at the beginning of her career. When she was shown into his office, his black brogues were resting on the edge of his desk, while he tilted back in a swivel chair, talking on the phone. With a flick of his hand, and the slightest nod, he indicated that she should sit down in the small armchair on the other side of his desk.

'Robert Mapplethorpe's work is the Parthenon of sado-masochistic homosexuality,' he said down the phone.

There was a pause. He looked over at Katherine incredulously; inviting her to marvel at the stupidity of the protests she could not hear.

'I could find you ten thousand sadists this afternoon,' he replied.

Further scepticism must have been expressed on the other end of the phone.

'Uptown or downtown?' said John, with a peal of knowing laughter.

While the conversation unfolded, Katherine found herself fascinated by Elton's disastrous hair transplant. She had been told about this radical new procedure but had never witnessed its results. The skin around the last fertile follicles had been cut from the back of his neck and sewn on to the hairless dome of his head. The raw red patches of stitched skin formed little islands of dying hair in a shining ocean of baldness.

John hung up the phone, with a contemptuous smirk.

'They buy a million-dollar book and they don't even know how to market it,' he said.

'Fools,' said Katherine, smiling.

'Do you have something for me?'

'I have the first half of my second novel,' said Katherine bashfully, taking a manila envelope from her plastic duty free bag.

'I loved *Hanging On Every Word*,' said John, and then bewitched her with his detailed knowledge of her first book.

Nothing had come of that New York meeting. She had waited a fortnight for his response to her typescript, and although he had told her that it was 'superb material', intoxicating her for a whole day, he had not, in the end, found a publisher who would commit to it in advance. They had drifted apart, as people do when they promise to stay in touch; the ones who are going to stay in touch don't need to promise. She knew that he was back in touch with her now because the stench of disappointment surrounding the Elysian debacle had reached his sensitive olfactory system. Her own agent, Angela, was completely blameless in the matter and Katherine had no intention of getting rid of her. In fact, Angela had written a fierce letter to the committee requesting that they take *Consequences* into consideration and explaining Page and Turner's mistake, but she had received a firm refusal from David Hampshire, saying that 'a deadline is a deadline', and that he was not going to 'open the floodgates to special pleading'. Given that she wasn't going to change agents, Katherine felt a certain apathy about taking up John's offer of lunch.

Besides, there had already been enough bloodletting, with the sacking of Alan's assistant and then of

Alan himself. She had almost written to him, but had managed to refrain. When she first cut a lover out of her life, she liked to do it thoroughly. Nevertheless, she felt something other than pure relief when Alan stopped writing to her, especially when Sam stopped at about the same time. And then, last night, after almost three weeks of silence she had received an email, not just from Sam but also about Alan and the shocking state he had been in when Sam ran into him in a shop in Pimlico. She hadn't answered him and she wasn't going to, at least not yet. The priority was to get rid of Didier, not to take back Sam or Alan.

She already knew what to expect from Didier as an ex-lover. When they had last separated he sent her emails that were little essays on the changing meaning of romantic and erotic love since the eighteenth century, indistinguishable from his published work, and indeed, after taking out the 'dear Katherines', he had published them.

And there he was again next door printing out more of his effortlessly opinionated prose. Katherine realized that she must get out of the flat as soon as possible. Perhaps she should ring John Elton after all and take him up on lunch. The fact that she would be immune to any of his advances now struck her as an advantage. She noticed yet again her loyalty to Angela and to her women friends in general, and its contrast with the ruthlessness of her behaviour towards men. In the Dodge City of romantic love, crowded with betrayal, abandonment and rejection, it was better to fire first than to take the risk of being gunned down. She felt the rapid pulse, the metallic taste, and the little razor cuts of the paranoid mentality that lay behind the apparent suavity and dominance of her love life. It suddenly horrified her that she couldn't send a kind word to Alan, who had lived with her and left his wife for her, and who was clearly falling apart, but she couldn't bear to linger on her remorse or her vulnerability for long, and so she threw off the bedclothes and got up briskly, determined to leave the flat as soon as possible.

17

Penny was on her way to Debenhams to buy an Extra Large Kettle. The Extra Large Kettle (or ELK) had been one of her main innovations at the Foreign Office. Even some members of the old guard, who had taken a sceptical, not to say frankly hostile view of her promotions during David Hampshire's time, were forced to admit that an extra cup of tea could make all the difference to a meeting that started out looking as if it might be very sticky indeed. She had a hunch that an ELK would be just as great an asset in the literary arena as it had proved to be in the foreign policy field, with many an Elysian meeting brightened by a seemingly inexhaustible supply of piping hot builder's tea.

With the pressure of so many books to read, Penny had decided to buy the audio versions of the

Long Listers she hadn't got round to, and listen to them being read by an actor with a lovely famous voice. As she downloaded *wot u starin at* and *The Greasy Pole* onto her poor overburdened iPad, she was reminded of a heart-breaking photograph she had once seen advertising a charity for maltreated Spanish donkeys. The dear little thing in the photo, thin as a stick, had been carrying burdens three times her own bulk, back and forth along dusty Spanish roads, until Donkey Rescue saved her from her cruel owner, renamed her Lollipop, and allowed her to end her days in donkey heaven, on a lovely farm run by a thoroughly practical English spinster who had retired to Andalusia. Penny had been so moved that she sent in a cheque for five pounds.

Although she didn't like the sound of *A Year in the Wild*, she was doing the responsible thing and had it in the passenger seat next to her, being given a chance. Her appetite for people, like the hero of this novel, who chose to live on roots and berries, was strictly limited. Some practical part of her wanted to send him down to M&S Simply Food to get one of their excellent ready-made meals. She was always delighted to see grizzly bears salmon-fishing in one of David Attenborough's splendid nature films, but she drew the line at grizzly bears lumbering into a novel in order to turn bankers into noble savages.

As a responsible driver, Penny always gave her full attention to the task at hand. Consequently, it wasn't until she came to a long queue of traffic approaching Marble Arch that she finally gave herself permission to listen to the rather hypnotic rendering of *A Year in the Wild*.

As spring returned to the frozen land, the great thaw began. It bewildered Gary with its clamour and its swiftness. The grey branches outside the cabin's southern window had hardly cast off their high narrow walls of snow, before they started to break out in bright green leaf. As soon as patches of ice melted on the lake, honking Canada geese landed on the fresh stretches of open water. The frozen stream he had crunched across in his snowshoes a few weeks before was transformed into an uproarious torrent that could only be forded by the big rock, or the Lynx Rock as he had named it in January. He had met a lynx there, completely still beside the rock, its triangular ears sharpening its attentiveness. What made it stand out against the snow was the fresh blood on the light brown fur around its mouth. He

*had stared at the lynx, and the lynx had stared back
at him, with the calm savagery of its yellow eyes;
animal to animal, predator to predator; he with a
dead hare in his game bag and the lynx with a dead
hare at its feet; his breath and the lynx's breath
steaming in the crystal silence of the northern woods.*

Oh, do get on with it, thought Penny. All this
description was driving her potty. The author clearly
had a bad case of the Doctor Dolittles, starting to
talk to the animals because he had turned his back
on his fellow man. If there was one thing Penny was
sure of it was this: man is a social animal through
and through, and nothing could be gained, except a
reputation for eccentricity, by cutting yourself off
from the rest of the human race. That was why she
was on her way to Debenhams to buy an Extra Large
Kettle, rather than chatting to a herd of caribou in
the wastes of northern Canada. She fast forwarded to
the next chapter, but missed the beginning because
she was now being swept along by the traffic rushing
around Marble Arch.

Soon enough, there was another jam waiting for
her at the beginning of Oxford Street and she was
forced to listen to more of Jo's exasperating novel.

. . . the yarrow with its feathery white and pink flowers and the bright red berries of the poisonous baneberry bush . . .

Oh, for heaven's sake, thought Penny, more description. She fast-forwarded again, just to confirm her suspicions, but her mind was made up: the author had written a guidebook to the fauna and flora of the Canadian outback, without the slightest concession to a novel's need for fast action and cliff-hanging suspense.

He drank the cool water from the swift-running stream and then lay back refreshed in the tall scratchy grass. A peregrine falcon circled above and then came out of its gliding motion and began to hover, holding its position above the ground with the scooping beat of its wings. Gary knew it had spotted its prey moving on the shore of the lake, and he felt his own body grow tense with anticipation as he stretched out his mind and merged it with the peregrine's perspective.

Dear, oh dear. Penny could only hope there was an adequate cottage hospital nearby where Gary could get the help he needed before he completely lost the plot.

'Excuse me; I think I'm a peregrine falcon,' she said, staring, wild-eyed into the rear-view mirror, and allowing herself a burst of derisive laughter.

So much for *A Year in the Wild*. As to *Outrage*, another one of Jo's Long Listers, once she had read the synopsis, Penny decided that she wasn't going to listen to it. It was written from the point of view of an eight-year-old boy living in a Johannesburg slum on the eve of South African independence. After his father is shot dead by a white policeman, the poor boy watches his mother being killed by the gang that has just raped her. He loses the power of speech but his 'traumatized stream of consciousness is a powerful meditation on the politics of gender, race and African identity'. All very impressive no doubt, but frankly life was quite depressing enough without listening to a story like that, which didn't even have the merit of being factually true.

When Penny arrived back at her flat with her magnificent new Kettle, she couldn't face listening to any more books, and yet the Elysian Prize still cast a shadow over the rest of her day, not just because she was off to dinner with Malcolm at the House of

Commons, but also because of a recent incident that had left her somewhat shaken. A few days earlier, a diarist from a very well-known national newspaper had rung to ask what she felt about the 'universal hostility' to the Long List. Penny kept as cool as a cucumber and pointed out that during her days at the Foreign Office, she had got quite used to dealing with trouble spots and dissenting voices. And then, in order to counteract any impression of being stuck up, she emphasized the ordinary side of her life by adding, 'I always had my daughter to go home to and help me keep my feet firmly on the ground.' It frankly defied belief that the diarist had gone on to contact Nicola to get her side of the story.

'She may have had me to go home to, but she was never at home when I got there,' Nicola was quoted as saying. 'Her feet were too firmly on the ground in her office, or at an independence ceremony in the middle of nowhere, or sucking up to the Americans at some conference. I hardly ever saw her, and even in her retirement she makes sure she's too busy to do anything useful.'

Penny was lost for words when she read these remarks. That your own flesh and blood should find it necessary to be so unkind and unfair in public took her breath away. If anything should take place behind closed doors, it was cruelty and betrayal.

After the initial sting, Penny set about wondering how she could repair relations with Nicola, who had always been hot-headed and was only lashing out because of the babysitting incident last month. Then Penny had a brainwave. There had been such a lot in the press about the odds betting shops were putting on the various novels, why not get Nicola to place a bet, not for Penny, of course, which would have been highly unethical, but for herself? She knew that Kentish Town needed a new roof, and a hot tip would have the further advantage of proving that Penny had no hard feelings about Nicola's unforgivable treachery. It also removed the moral pressure on Penny to dig into her savings in order to protect her nearest and dearest from the elements. At 30–1 *wot u starin at* was pretty irresistible for someone who knew that it was one of the chairman's favourites, and that he was a singularly impressive man whom Penny intended to support in every way she could.

18

Why should Sam let Katherine ruin his love for her? Did love have to disappear with her disappearance? Did he have to hate love because it wasn't working out the way he wanted? Since he was going to think about her all day, one way or another, why not think about her as he always had, from the first time she sat next to him by chance at a concert, wearing a pair of faded pink tennis shoes and a soft blue overcoat, her hair still beaded with rain? The concert became the soundtrack of their proximity, the slightest pressure from her sleeve made him feel that his body was interfusing with hers and that he had been waiting all his life for this union.

It was hard not to react, not to feel humiliated by a unilateral longing, not to let pathology creep, like a mist under the door, into his reading of the situation.

Despair was a worthy adversary, luring him towards contempt for Katherine, or jealousy of Didier, or pity for himself. The antidote to despair was not optimism – optimism was its staple diet, making him hope for something that was not the case and driving him back to despair. The only antidote was to embrace the despair and remain in love, to give the phrase 'hopelessly in love' its true meaning.

Why dim the lights when he really needed to tear down the grid? What was the use of having a drink, or going to an afternoon film, or catching a train, or going to bed with another woman, or being proud or being angry? Instead, when he was surfeited with Katherine's absence and would rather have set fire to the curtains than go on thinking about it, he stayed a little longer in its ruthless company. Not to shut down, not to run away: that was his job, to stay open even when love took the form of pain. It had taken him this long to be wholehearted, and whatever Katherine did he was not going to retreat from that bewilderingly private victory.

He continued to communicate with her, without her. Just as reassuring the patient that he has no legs cannot cure the pain in a phantom limb, it was no use trying to stop Sam from speaking to Katherine just because she wasn't in the room and couldn't hear anything he said. He told her that his feelings for her had not become twisted or complicated, but were like a paused film that would resume exactly where she had left it, even if she took five or ten years to come back.

He found that he had been heated beyond his melting point by romantic love and, although it had failed, it still left him inclined to rush towards other kinds of love more readily than before. When he saw the news and heard the widow of a policeman, shot in Northern Ireland by the 'Continuity IRA', say that her husband had been a 'good man' and that her life was 'ruined' by his death, he burst into tears, watching carefully to see if his grief was exploiting hers. Instead, to his horror, he saw that his tears were the only natural response to her suffering, and to the suffering of the men who had killed her husband, and that he had spent his life defended against compassion by a practical and robust selfishness that would soon callous his responses again, if he allowed it to. The next morning he saw a child being dragged to school a little too roughly by a harassed mother, his tumbling steps hardly able to keep up with her hurried strides, and it was all he could do not to intervene.

He stopped and stared at the mother a little madly, hoping she would wake up to what she was doing and treat the child more gently. In that case, he felt that his response was much more impure than it had been with the widow, more tangled up with the desire for the woman who had power over his happiness to treat him more gently, but the underlying truth was intact: every kind of cruelty was unbearable to someone who refused, or failed, to shut down.

For a writer as resolute as Sam, it was unimaginable that his intense misery would not be material for writing, and unimaginable that it would. Maybe in order to be material later on he had to accept that it was not material now. Maybe he had to be patient, to 'recollect in tranquillity' in the Wordsworthian manner, and not to take notes on every species of flower he was trampling underfoot, in the manner Wordsworth despised. Or maybe it would never be material. The rawness could not be written about without betraying its essence. He was not going to cover it with layer after nacreous layer of aesthetic distance; pain was pain, not a pearl in waiting. It was indecent to think he could make anything of it, and so he left his notebooks unopened and his lovesick journal unwritten.

19

John Elton was having lunch in Claridge's.

'You're being too modest,' he said, 'my informants tell me that it's a great deal more than a cookbook.'

'Well,' said Auntie, playing with the folds of her sari to cover her growing mystification at the fuss being made about her book, 'people seem to think that it has some literary merit.'

'A great deal of literary merit,' said John, with a powerful charismatic smile. He turned to include the nephew, but Sonny remained slumped in his armchair, hidden behind a huge pair of dark glasses. 'I can't tell you how I know this,' John continued, 'but I've been told by an impeccable source that your book is going to be on the Short List. Please don't tell anyone.'

This was pure invention, but either it would turn out to be true, enhancing his reputation for prescience, or he would not take on Auntie as a client and nobody, except for these obscure Indian grandees, would know that his prophecy had failed.

'But it's a prize for the art of fiction . . .' said Auntie, faltering in the face of these further honours.

'Including fiction artfully disguised as culinary fact,' said John, beaming.

'I simply sent my secretary to ask our old cook in Badanpur, who naturally can't write, to recite the recipes that have been passed down through the generations.'

John Elton let out a gust of confident laughter, as if he were starring in an advertisement for a new mouthwash. There was no doubt that Auntie's supercilious manner would have to be carefully managed. Just as Magritte hid his surrealism under the uniform of the Belgian Bourgeoisie, India's Lawrence Sterne takes a mischievous pleasure in playing the *grande dame*. She appears to get her secretary to 'write' a 'cookbook' in order to challenge our expectations about the nature of authorship – something like that might work.

'I hope you can keep this up in the interviews,' he

said. 'It's superb: the illiteracy that engenders literature; the rhetoric that denies rhetoric; "I will a round unvarnished tale deliver", as Othello says, before speaking some of the most beautiful English ever written. And the narrative frames: the secretary who interviews the cook – the man on the quayside who knows a story about the Congo; the man on the coach who could tell you a tale about the Caucasus. Superb!'

'I'm not following you,' said Auntie, irritably.

'Well,' said John, with the air of a man who is playing along with an entertaining masquerade, 'at least you'll admit that it's an *unusual* cookbook.'

This simplified formula gave Auntie some relief.

'Of course, it's *unusual*,' she said. 'It's full of wonderful anecdotes, family portraits, and recipes that have been jealously guarded for centuries.'

'Wonderful. Would it be possible to see a copy?' asked John, who was more used to being burdened with manuscripts than pleading to see one.

'The only copy in England was brought here by Miss Katherine Burns, a friend of my nephew's. She's done so much more than we expected. I keep asking Sonny to invite her to lunch, but he hasn't been able to arrange anything yet.'

'Oh, I know Katherine,' said John, 'we had lunch only the other day. I'd be happy to set something up.' He tried smiling again at Sonny, but the nephew remained slouched unresponsively in his chair.

'Thank you,' said Auntie graciously. 'I'll get my secretary to send you a copy of the book.'

'I can't wait to read it,' said John. 'Playing with textuality can be dangerous, but the audacity of putting it in a "cookbook" is sheer genius.'

'I suppose so . . .' Auntie hesitated. She couldn't help feeling that if she was going to have a literary agent, it would be better if she had some idea of what he was talking about.

'Let's face it, Auntie,' said Sonny, suddenly bursting in on the conversation with undisguised bitterness, 'you're a big-time literary success.'

'Sonny has,' Auntie found herself wanting to say 'also', but resisted, 'written a novel, but I'm afraid it's been overlooked by the committee – most unfairly.'

'Quite,' said Sonny. 'But since there is no interest in representing *my* work, I will leave you to have lunch together on your own.'

'On the contrary, I had no idea . . .' John began, but Sonny turned away too vehemently for him to finish his sentence.

Overhearing his aunt's sad reflection that he'd 'always been oversensitive, even as a little boy', only added to Sonny's contempt and fury as he stormed away. Auntie was taking the side of that American agent against her own nephew! Elton hadn't once mentioned *The Mulberry Elephant*; in fact, he behaved as if he had never heard of it! He was too busy sucking up to Auntie, just because she was going to be on the Short List. Sonny had a good mind to get Mansur to finish him off as well, but despite these strong impulses he was too disciplined to lose sight of his primary target.

He had to admit that part of his outrage over the American had been manufactured so that he could get away and at last discuss with Mansur how to dispose of Malcolm Craig, MP. To maintain his little fiction about an agonizing back pain, Sonny had been carried around a good deal by the turbaned brute over the last five days, but somehow it never seemed to be the right moment to make his special request. Now, with his pride freshly stung by that humiliating lunch, he thought he might finally be ready to cut through the awkwardness of asking a servant to step beyond the strict limits of his job description and assassinate an enemy on his master's behalf.

20

Didier watched as coffee trickled from the espresso machine in Katherine's kitchen into a tiny cup resting on the metal grille beneath. Knowing that the fourth espresso was usually the one to tip him into a frenzy of creativity, he knocked back the bitter little draft while it was still steaming, placed the cup directly in the sink, and returned with relish, and a slightly burnt mouth, to his computer. Katherine was out for the day, giving him the further impetus of solitude.

He was soon typing rapidly, thrilled by the intelligence and authority of the words rippling onto the screen.

Nietzsche announced the death of God; Foucault announced the death of Man; the death of Nature announces itself, with no need for an intermediary.

As these three elements of our classical discourse dissolve in the acid rain of late Capitalism, we are offered the consolation of its own pale triumvirate: the producer, the consumer and the commodity. Thanks to advertising, the producer sells the commodity to the consumer; thanks to the Internet, the consumer is the commodity sold to the producer. This is the Utopia of borderless democracy: a shift of signifier in the desert of the Real. This is the playground of unlimited freedom: the opportunity to define ourselves through the gratification of an ever more perverse and hybridized fetishism. This is the celebrated openness of a technology that is at the service of perpetual supervision. It is this 'open' field that is the supreme disguise: in the absence of the hidden object, we cannot see what we see, because we have abandoned the need to search. As for searching, let our engines do it for us! The thought that cannot think itself is that we will die of thirst before we reach the shining city of individual gratification, which was never made of anything other than the shimmering heat waves of a collectively conditioned desire.

In the rhetoric of bourgeois liberalism, conformity deploys the language of rebellion, precisely because *there is no possibility of revolution. We are at the point in history where it is easier to imagine the end of the world than the end of Capitalism. The anxiety once expended on the mutual annihilation of warring political ideologies is now expended on universal annihilation through ecological catastrophe; preferably, of course, a catastrophe that is not going to happen, rather than the one that is happening. We would rather watch a movie about the threat of a meteor from outer space than contemplate the actual impact of the Capitalist meteor on the Earth. We may be frivolous consumers of information, who cannot stop eating popcorn until the US Air Force has saved humanity by destroying the alien meteor with nuclear weapons, or we may be serious consumers of information, who enjoy the voluptuous guilt of betraying the polar bear, or worry that our grandchildren may never know the pleasures of skiing in the Alps, or wish we had bought an apartment on a higher floor of the Manhattan sky-scraper where we live. Finally, it is of no importance, because both catastrophes, the fantastic and the actual, are deployed to distract us from the desert of the Real into which we have marched the exhausted culture of the West. In this desert, it is forbidden to think.*

Even if Capitalism is the crisis, Capitalism must be the solution!

Didier paused, waiting for a second preposterous paradox to pop into his head. He was *en pleine forme*, no doubt about that. Would another espresso send him spiralling into a circular but inconclusive sterility, or keep him riding on the rushing and glittering wave of *La Pensée*? Before he could decide, the ping of an incoming email drew his attention to the lower corner of the screen. He would usually have ignored an email in the midst of writing, but this one was from Katherine and might require a quick reply. He clicked on his Mail icon and read her message.

Didier, you'll probably think me very cowardly to tell you this by email, but I don't feel that I can go on being with you. I know this is the second time and that you'll think I shouldn't have taken you back if I wasn't serious, but my restlessness is, as you might say, structural and not personal. I would have left whoever I was with at this point, because I need continual change to keep me ahead of the wolf pack – whatever that is.

*I am going to Italy with a (girl) friend for two
weeks. I have an inkling of a new novel, and
want to see if I can start it there. You're welcome
to stay in the flat until I get back.*

*Please forgive me, and don't cut me off from
your wonderful company, unless you have to.*

Love, K

Didier felt the glittering wave collapse around him
and found himself tumbling and spinning, and struggling to know which way was up. How could she do
that? How could she suddenly do that?

He thought of Lacan's opaque but strangely com-
pelling remark: 'Woman does not exist, which does
not mean that she cannot be the object of desire'.
Whatever charm this insight had once held for him,
it slipped through his grasp as he groped for a sane
response to Katherine's email.

She had ruined a day's writing. That, at least, was
a concrete starting point for his resentment. Mercifully, his focus on lost writing reminded him that
he would one day infold his present suffering into
a masterful analysis of Desire, or Love, or Delusion;
it hardly mattered: he would perform a vivisection
without anaesthetic on any abstract nouns that pre-

sumed to rule his life. He knew it would be some time before he could gather enough detachment for that task. Rome wasn't deconstructed in a day, he thought, immediately typing the sentence on to his screen, to see if he felt the return of some measure of control. He did not.

Didier got up from his desk and suddenly swept the coffee cup from its ledge of papers, smashing it against the wall of Katherine's drawing room. He would have his revenge, he didn't yet know what it would be, but he would write something about Love, or Delusion, or Desire that she would never forget. As this thought died out, Didier pictured himself sweeping the coffee cup against the wall, and suspected there was something staged about the gesture. Yes, he had been in the stupidity of his unconscious and its mechanical discharge of emotion. He wished he could have the cup back, so that he could experience the full tension between the gestural cliché and the more subtle and refreshing operations of his intellect, and then refuse the gesture. He sat down again and typed out a sentence.

Impulsiveness always points to the absence of spontaneity.

That was better; he could work with that.

In the meantime, he had joined Sam and Alan in Katherine's *salon des refusés*. Would he try to preserve the dignity of having lasted a few more weeks than either of his rivals, or join them in an enclave of nostalgia and bitterness? There were several emails from Sam he had not answered, because of the danger of being unavoidably (or structurally, as Katherine would want him to say, so as to enforce the tyranny of English facetiousness) patronizing. He might now be able to reply to Sam, but first he would reply to Katherine.

Didier got up again and started pacing the room. 'The wolf pack' she was keeping ahead of, that was the way in. He felt the richness of its hermeneutic potential. Once he started interpreting something, the problem was how to stop. All he needed was a first sentence, and one more espresso.

21

Malcolm had insisted that Tobias attend the meeting to decide the Short List, and when he arrived he was an object of great curiosity, not only for his novelty but also for his annoying good looks, which had an immediate and evident impact on the three female members of the committee. His long hair, long scarf and long overcoat emphasized his tallness, and left Malcolm feeling small and portly, as well as jealous. He was determined to hide these feelings behind a show of warmth and cordiality, since he wanted to be able to count on Tobias's vote as well as Penny's.

After the introductions and the greetings, the meeting got off to a surprisingly acrimonious start with Vanessa immediately going on the attack with the ridiculous claim that *The Palace Cookbook* wasn't a novel at all. Although Malcolm had not

yet got round to reading it, he knew that the distinguished old firm of Page and Turner would not have
sent in a book that wasn't a novel, nor was Jo likely
to be so confused that she couldn't tell a novel from
a cookbook. In any case, Jo turned out to have an
impressive command of all the right jargon.

'I'm surprised that you don't recognize its qualities,' she said to Vanessa. 'You claim to be an expert
on contemporary fiction and yet, faced with a ludic,
postmodern, multi-media masterpiece, you naively
deny that it's a novel at all.'

'It's not a novel,' said Vanessa, 'it's a cookbook.
It's called *The Palace Cookbook* because it's a cookbook.' She let out a growl of childish fury.

'It tells the story of a family,' said Jo, admirably
calm under fire, 'through cooking. What could be
more universal, after all, than the language of food?'

'Inuit, Catalan, Gaelic, *any* fucking language,' said
Vanessa, 'because food isn't a language, it's something
you eat.'

'There's no need to use that sort of tone,' said
Penny. She'd had just about enough of Vanessa's
effing and blinding.

'On the contrary,' said Vanessa, 'I have no choice,

because I'm talking to people who are immune to argument and have no idea how to read a book.'

'I *loved* the chicken curry with lime and cardamom,' said Tobias, disarming the warring Amazons with his languid charm. Underneath his overcoat, which he had discarded in a window seat, he turned out to be wearing a faded purple T-shirt, frayed jeans and a pair of battered cowboy boots.

'Well, there you are,' said Jo. 'It's important that it works at a "realistic" level, while simultaneously operating as the boldest metafictional performance of our time.'

Malcolm, slightly irritated by Tobias's soothing impact on the women, couldn't help challenging him a little too sharply on which books he thought should be on the Short List. Tobias leant back, sweeping the hair from his forehead and gazing at the ceiling, and then with no more introduction than a sudden return to an upright position, and an open-handed gesture, he began to recite in a rich mellow voice.

'*There was scarce a lad in all of Warwickshire more comely than young Master William, with the tresses of his hair, dark as the raven's wing, tumbling almost to his shoulders, and his cheeks like a pair of ripe English apples, and his eyes as blue as a summer's day, only more lovely and more temperate. She might be no more than his nurse, but young Rosalind could have sworn by the Holy Body of Our Saviour that she loved William as much as ever a mother loved her own child. That morning she had bought him an orange in the market place without her mistress's permission, and she feared lest she be chided for a wanton spendthrift, but she had only done it to show little William what a wondrous fruit it was, and to tell him how clever men in Italy had discovered that the whole world was round, just like an orange, only different in size and colour.*

Comparing one thing with another was one of William's favourite games. Many's the time the two of them had tarried in the damp grass, under the ever changing sky, gazing at the great clouds, like bur- nished galleons sailing through the bright flood of the firmament, and Master William would say, 'How like a camel, sweet Rosalind,' and she would say, 'Most like a camel, Master William,' and then he would say, 'Methinks 'tis more like a towered citadel than a camel,' and she would say, 'Most like, my love,' not wanting to contradict him in the smallest wise, but wanting to make sure that he loved and trusted the unparagoned treasure of his green imagination.'

'Magical,' said Tobias, 'absolutely magical.'

'Fancy being able to remember all that,' said Penny.

'And what about *The Greasy Pole?*' said Malcolm.

'Oh, it has my vote,' said Tobias.

'Good,' said Malcolm.

'And I'm blown away by *wot u starin at*,' said Tobias, 'fascinating, harrowing and fiercely original.'

'It certainly isn't original,' said Vanessa, 'it's just sub-Irvine Welsh.'

'It's relevant, Vanessa. Re-le-vant,' said Jo.

'I prefer revelatory,' said Vanessa.

'Why? Because it's got more syllables?'

Penny let out an involuntary guffaw.

'Your problem, Vanessa,' said Malcolm, 'is that it's not a novel about a middle-class family whose worst nightmare is that they might have to take little Bertie and Fiona out of their fee-paying schools because Daddy didn't get his obscene Christmas bonus from the bank this year.'

'Spare us the class warrior,' said Vanessa, 'especially when you have a car waiting outside to take you back to your Georgian house in Barton Street. The measure of a work of art is how much art it has in it, not how much "relevance". Relevant to whom? Relevant to what? Nothing is more ephemeral than a hot topic.'

Malcolm felt it was time to defuse the atmosphere with a cup of tea. He had feigned delight before the beginning of the meeting when Penny presented him with a gigantic caterer's kettle he could barely imagine lifting when it was empty, let alone after it was loaded with gallons of boiling water, but now he was grateful to be able to get up from the conference table and occupy himself with making the tea. The simple change of position made him feel more like an informed eavesdropper than the chairman of the board. He could hear Vanessa's exasperation as she gradually realized that the majority of her so-called 'literary' novels were not going to make it on to the Short List. She kept trying to argue that the other novels lacked the qualities that characterized a work of literature: 'depth, beauty, structural integrity, and an ability to revive our tired imaginations with the precision of its language'. The poor woman didn't seem to realize that what counted in the adult world was working out compromises between actual members of a committee that reflected the forces at work in the wider society, like Parliament in relation to the nation as a whole. Vanessa had taken on the role of a doomed backbencher, making speeches to an empty chamber about values that simply had no place in the modern world. Frankly, he felt rather sorry for her. However, he started to focus more keenly when they came round to *The Bruce* and he heard her claim that it was more or less plagiarized from an obscure Edwardian novel called *The Tartan King*.

'All he's done is update some of the diction, and spice up the plot with a few scenes stolen from *Braveheart*,' said Vanessa.

'Ah, *Braveheart*,' said Tobias, slipping effortlessly into a Scottish accent. '*Aye, fight and you may die; run and you will live, at least a while. And dying in your beds many years from now, would you be willing to trade all the days, from this day to that, for one chance, just one chance to come back here and tell our enemies that they can take our lives, but they can never take our freedom!*' Tobias let loose a rousing cheer from an imaginary army of blue-faced warriors. 'Terrific stuff,' he added.

'Thank you, Tobias, for reminding us of a scene

which, if memory serves, is not in *The Bruce*,' said Malcolm, struggling to tilt the unwieldy kettle over the edge of a teapot. 'I don't know if you're aware of it, Vanessa,' he went on, 'but all of Shakespeare's plots are lifted wholesale from other sources, and I haven't heard any complaints about *his* work recently. I admire your idealism, but I'm sorry to say, there's nothing new under the sun.'

'There's certainly nothing new about that expression,' said Vanessa. 'But that's the whole point, if a writer can't cut through the half-truths and lazy assumptions of cliché and platitude, then he can't make a work of art. We don't care about Shakespeare's derivative plots because he transforms them with the brilliant originality of his language.'

'Personally,' said Tobias, 'I agree. If this imposter didn't write the book, I don't see why we should give him the prize.'

Malcolm, who had been smiling sadly but indulgently at Vanessa's misguided views, allowed a frown to darken his face. He lifted the brimming teapot with both hands and started to carry it, somewhat stiffly, towards the conference table.

Jo, who had been oddly silent until that moment, suddenly saw her opportunity and spoke up.

'Absolutely,' she said, in her most matter-of-fact tone, as if she had no personal investment in the outcome. 'I'm afraid that I agree with Vanessa and Tobias on this one. We will have to rule out *The Bruce*. It simply isn't fair on the candidates who've written their own novels to include a writer who's copied out someone else's.'

'Unbelievable!' muttered Malcolm, jerking his hands upwards in a reflexive gesture of protest.

Penny later told him that she could remember every detail with dreamlike clarity: the scalding tea spilling onto Malcolm's hands, his cry of pain, the teapot flying through the air and smashing against the fireplace, its shards scattering in every direction and the dark brew splashing onto the fake logs and soaking the beige carpet.

The meeting, like the teapot, soon broke up and dispersed. The Short List was not yet finalized, but it was getting late, the atmosphere was strained, and everyone agreed to continue the process by email.

One thing about choosing the best novel of the year had become absolutely clear to Malcolm: Jo must be stopped at any cost. Her stranglehold over the Short List was truly scandalous. He reinvigorated his alliance with Penny on the phone later that evening. She felt the same way about Jo's growing power and they agreed that after reading her choices they would compare notes over dinner and see which of her novels most deserved to be attacked.

22

As Alan spread the thick foam on his grey-flecked beard, he realized how much he had been missing the sanity and dullness of what Henry James had perhaps exaggerated in calling 'the joy of the matutinal steel'. Compared to the lacerating edge of his unhappiness over the last month, his razor blade felt like the stroke of a feather as it scraped its way through the thickets of obstinate stubble covering his face.

Why had he woken this morning, shaken and weak, but somehow determined to stop his decline – and to shave? Was it the lure of a small but uncontested area of self-determination? No employer was going to sack him for shaving; no woman was going to tell him that, although she hoped they would remain friends, she didn't want to go on shaving with him any more. With the exhilaration of a pioneer taming the wilderness, he saw fresh tracks of skin opening across his face. He shook his blade under the running water and reapplied it expertly to his chin. This face was his face, from shining ear to shining ear, from the ridge of his upper lip to the bulge of his Adam's apple, from the clean line of his manly jaw to the disappointing looseness of his double chin. He dried himself carefully. There were no cuts, or neglected patches of beard; every movement showed that he knew what he was doing, that he was a man who could be trusted.

Yesterday, he had written to his old acquaintance James Miller at IPG, the talent agency, and asked for some work, any work. He wasn't expecting to be treated like the senior editor he had been at Page and Turner. He could work for a trial period, read from the slush pile, write rejection letters, or try to lure some of his old authors over to the agency. James had replied with an email, both buoyant and cautious, accompanied by the promise of three typescripts that had 'made it out of the slush pile but not yet been read by an editor'. Alan was tidying himself up to meet these harbingers of a return to productive life. No more sprawling around in his narrow room in acrid pyjamas, with the medicinal fumes of cheap vodka rising from his cup of morning tea. There may have been no mention of money in James's email, but Alan was being given a chance, and that would have to do for now. Besides, the weakness of his position, as well as the gentlemanly mist that still lingered over the field of publishing, made it impossible for Alan to demand any clarification, let alone money.

As he put on his clean white shirt, mildly puzzled that he was dressing to meet some almost certainly unpublishable typescripts, he realized that he hadn't taken any trouble over his appearance since the day he left Katherine's flat. He was not just dressing for work; he was defying her rejection for the first time. All he had to do was make a clean break between what Katherine thought of him and what he thought of himself. Maybe depression was always a matter of taking on a hostile point of view that, however intimate it might seem, was essentially alien. We were not put on this earth to hate ourselves, thought Alan, doing up the waistband of his trousers as if to secure this merciful claim; it's always an unnatural state of affairs, however irresistible it seems at the time.

He had to admit that his meeting with Sam and Didier had contributed to his recovery, even if that hadn't been immediately obvious. Sam had first spotted him halfway through the month, staring at the last three bottles of Dostoyevsky vodka in the local corner shop. Thanks to its resemblance to a batch of bootleg paraffin, Dostoyevsky was already the cheapest vodka on the shelf, but on this particular day a fluorescent green star announced a special offer that further lowered the price by two pounds. Alan could hardly believe his luck as he grabbed the dusty bottles and rolled them clinking into his wire basket. He was dismayed to be interrupted by Sam, a man he hardly knew and in any case associated with the woman whose memory he was trying to obliterate. Sam was clearly shocked by his derelict state, but Alan soon shook him off and hurried back to the hermitage of his darkened room in the Mount Royal. He forgot about Sam long before he had absorbed enough Dostoyevsky to forget about Katherine's limbs and lips.

It had only been three days ago, when he couldn't bear his loneliness any longer and caved in to Sam's offer of lunch, that Alan learned he was not alone. In fact, he was rather put out by just how many lovers Katherine had managed to get rid of in the last month.

'No need to *cherchez la femme*,' said Didier, 'she has searched for us, like a heat-seeking missile!'

'Were you having an affair with her at the same time as me?' Alan asked.

'Yes,' said Sam.

'And at the same time as each other?'

'Very much so,' said Didier, 'it could not have been more simultaneous!'

'Good God,' said Alan, drinking half his glass of Chianti in a single gulp, 'this is the woman I left my wife for.'

'You had a wife and a mistress,' said Didier. 'She had three lovers. For us the problem is that she is a woman, but in India and Tibet . . .'

'I don't care about Tibet,' Alan interrupted him. 'Anyway, I *left* my wife for her. There was nothing simultaneous about it; well, at least not after I'd left Marilyn.'

'Typically,' said Didier, 'by now you will have asked her to take you back.'

Alan knocked back the rest of his Chianti, furious at being so obvious.

'This is not the time to be guilty about the pursuit of pleasure,' said Didier. 'Permissiveness is the only ideology we are permitted. We are not just allowed to enjoy anything; we are obliged to enjoy everything. Classically, the patient went into psychotherapy because she was neurotic from the suppression of her perverse desires; now she goes into psychotherapy because she is guilty about not enjoying her perverse desires: "Doctor, what's wrong with me? Why don't I want to tie up my boyfriend? Why can't I get in touch with my lesbian side?" Et cetera, et cetera.'

'I don't see what this has . . .' Alan tried to interject.

'Epicurus is bent over the handlebars of his pleasure machine, speeding along the Information Super Highway!' Didier continued unstoppably.

'I think we should narrow our focus,' Sam began.

'Finally,' said Didier, raising a warning finger. 'Finally, we realize that we have been quenching our thirst with seawater, and we decide to "*take back the power*". We are going to jog, meditate, et cetera, et cetera – but it's not so easy! We can't just sit at home meditating, which would cost nothing, and therefore make us very nervous. We must look for a teacher who lives in India, or California . . .'

'I'm sorry,' Alan finally managed, 'but what's all of this got to do with Katherine?'

'It has everything to do with all of us,' Didier

replied. 'This is the world-historical field through which the contemporary search for the truth must take its course.'

'But I loved her,' said Alan.

'Ah, love . . .' Didier began, 'when we speak of love . . .'

'Listen,' said Sam, placing a restraining hand on Didier's arm, 'I understand.'

'I wish you didn't understand, frankly,' said Alan, pushing back his chair with a sharp scraping sound from the tiled floor, 'since it means that you were fucking Katherine while we were living together.' He needed another pint of Dostoyevsky fairly urgently; the Chianti was just too slow and watery.

'But you were sleeping with Katherine while you were still living with your wife,' said Didier. 'You are trapped in the old paradigm of transgression when in reality . . .'

'Oh, fuck off,' said Alan. 'I don't know what world-historical field you were in when you planned this lunch, but it's not a world I live in, and this lunch is history.'

With these words, of which he was moderately proud and mildly ashamed, Alan left the restaurant.

It took him another day to realize that the pressure

on him had lessened. However annoyed he had been by the meeting, the logic of spreading a weight over a larger area had held. It was impossible to believe that Sam and Didier had suffered as much as him, but even the feeble support offered by their vaguely similar experiences gave him some relief. There was also a welcome splintering of his hostility, which had been almost exclusively directed against himself, with the odd burst of drunken rage towards Katherine and Yuri, but could now include Motor Mouth Didier and Philandering Sam among its targets.

The grey phone on his bedside table rang, taking Alan by surprise. Slobodan, the former Yugoslavian receptionist whose disdainful glances Alan had grown to dread, told him that a package was waiting for him downstairs. On his way out, Alan hooked his empty rucksack over his shoulder and checked himself in the mirror; amazed to see the return of the clean-shaven and unpretentiously dressed friend he had lost sight of a month ago.

He glided down the stairs he had so often stumbled down and as he arrived in the entrance, he took it in with a new kind of neutrality. The words 'Mount Royal', fixed to the fake wood casing of the reception desk, in big gold letters which used to fascinate him with their power to distort the arrival and departure of hotel guests and, in quiet moments, reflect the rippling passage of a red bus beyond the hotel's glass front door, now simply struck him as garish.

Slobodan acknowledged Alan's changed appearance by briefly raising an eyebrow to show that he was not so easily fooled. He handed over two canvas bags, which Alan couldn't resist glancing into immediately. In one was the familiar sight of two typescripts in transparent plastic folders. From the other Alan fished out a gigantic purple book covered in debossed golden domes and parapets. *The Mulberry Elephant* was written in rich orange calligraphic lettering across its front. On a note obscuring the name of the author, someone from IPG had written, 'Published In India – looking for publisher here'.

Alan decided to leave the intimidating volume in his room and take the intriguing typescripts with him to a cafe. He felt the visceral excitement that had kept him going as a publisher. Maybe these would turn out to be yet more disappointing and incompetent texts, but perhaps one of them was a masterpiece, or still better, something he could help turn into a masterpiece.

23

It was ironic, in Penny's opinion, that her slavish devotion to the cause of literature was preventing her from writing any more of her own novel. She was determined to spend the last twenty-four hours before the feeding frenzy of the Short List announcement doing some of her own work for a change.

Quite apart from their distracting quality, she was not at all pleased with the discourteous tone that had come to dominate the Elysian committee meetings. David Hampshire was taking her out to dinner that night and she was going to suggest a remedy. Last Sunday she had watched a thoroughly inspiring documentary about corporate bonding. It had followed two groups of colleagues, up a Norwegian fjord in one case, and across Dartmoor in the other, all being led by former SAS commandos. These young soldiers started out looking like strong silent types, but turned out to have thought long and hard about the value of getting back to basics and cultivating *esprit de corps*. Although there would not be time to spend a week on Dartmoor with three matches, a compass and a rabbit trap, or to go to Norway and enjoy the breath-taking natural scenery, howl at the moon, and gaze at the *aurora borealis*, she did intend to ask David to have a word with the Elysian Board and see if they would finance a trip to Paris with an overnight stay in a nice hotel.

Most people went to Paris to look at Impressionist paintings of holidaymakers lying around on a riverbank. What Penny had in mind was altogether more challenging: a good hard look at the infrastructure of the city. A limited public tour of the Paris sewers had been on offer for years, but Penny intended to use her Foreign Office contacts to get the committee taken through the entire system, led by a real expert, with a map of Paris showing them exactly what they were underneath at the time. The Louvre, the Opera House, the Comédie Française, whatever it might be, they would be seeing it from a point of view that very few people indeed had ever had the chance to enjoy.

EDWARD ST. AUBYN

That was tonight's task, but right now, it was time to get on with some writing.

Jane took a moment to assess her situation. It didn't look good. In fact, it couldn't have been much worse. She was in an isolated castle on the west coast of Sicily, without her mobile phone, hiding in an old oak cupboard with far from silent hinges, while the world's most dangerous terrorist took a shower in his en suite bathroom next door. It defied belief, but all the evidence pointed to the fact that the Russian oligarch and owner of the Villa Concerta, Vladimir Rhazin, was bankrolling Ibrahim al-Shukra's international terrorist network. The old Soviet cold-war game of destabilizing the West was clearly still part of Russia's foreign-policy agenda, even if the perpetrators were now disguised as some of the world's most avid consumers of Western decadence.

It was a distinctly odd feeling, Jane reflected grimly, to be in possession of such stunning intelligence, without knowing whether she would live long enough to pass it on to Thames House. One person she would certainly not be telling was Richard Lane. He would somehow claim all the glory for himself, while managing to reprimand her for burning the

160

rulebook. She had to admit that hiding in the freezing luggage hold of Rhazin's Falconer T 300, the most expensive executive jet on the market, with a price tag of forty-five million dollars, had been insanely risky, but if ever the motto 'Nothing ventured, nothing gained' had any meaning at all, it was now. If only she hadn't forgotten her BlackBerry in the glove compartment of her Audi 3.0 TDI, she could have sent a text to Peggy Fields right now, and got her to transfer it to her computer with a time code, so that Lane couldn't get his thieving hands on her intelligence.

Penny sank back into her button leather swivel chair. That was as far as she had got. What was going to happen next?

Jane winced as she opened the creaky old cupboard door.

Penny paused; she wanted to really give the reader a sense of how dramatic this moment was, really get the atmosphere across. She typed the word 'atmosphere' in the Gold Ghost Plus search box, and then changed it to 'air', which seemed to her more subtle and suggestive. Immediately, dozens of alternatives rippled on to the page.

> 'The bracing seaside air . . . the air, heavy with the scent of roses . . . the air was crackling with tension . . .'

That was it. She highlighted the last phrase, clicked, and Bob's your uncle.

The air was crackling with tension. Every nerve in her body was straining to hear the shower. While the water was still running she was safe. If it stopped, she would have to run back to the cupboard

The situation reminded Penny of something she couldn't quite put her finger on. Then she got it, and finished the sentence triumphantly.

in the most lethal game of Grandmother's Footsteps ever played.

She climbed carefully out of the cupboard and started to tiptoe her way across the vast room. When she was halfway across, the sound of running water suddenly stopped. Jane froze; she was as far from the cupboard as the door. What should she do? Using her woman's intuition, and her memories of a parachute-training course she'd been sent on when she had first joined the Service, she threw herself onto the floor and rolled smoothly under the giant Jacobean four poster bed recently purchased by Rhazin for a six-figure sum at Christie's, Geneva. She was panting like

Penny paused and closed her eyes waiting for inspiration.

a schoolgirl after a hockey match, but she had to force herself to breathe more quietly so she could concentrate on what was happening.

The shower door opening. Al-Shukra's singing growing louder. The last splashes of water from the showerhead. A sudden cry of alarm. A thud. A groan. Silence. Jane lay on the floor under the musty mattress for what seemed like an eternity. Then she lifted the velvet valence and peered across the room. Nothing stirred. Her heart was beating like a jackhammer in her chest. She wriggled out from under the bed, got to her feet and moved gingerly towards the bathroom door. The sight that greeted her was both horrifying and highly satisfactory. Al-Shukra was lying on the

white Carrera marble floor, a red stain spreading
slowly from the back of his head.

Gaining in confidence, Jane walked into the bath-
room. In the corner of the room she saw the glisten-
ing bar of Bulgari's Liaisons Dangereuses bath soap
that had quite literally caused al-Shukra's downfall.

'You think you're so clever,' said Jane, stand-
ing mockingly over al-Shukra's fallen body, 'sending
suicide bombers out to make cowardly attacks on
innocent members of the public, but you don't look
so clever now, do you?'

The phone rang, making Penny jump. She had
been so deeply engaged in her creation that she had
completely lost any sense of the outside world. She
answered the call reluctantly, feeling that her chapter
might be imperilled by this untimely interruption.

'Hi, Mum, it's Nicola.'

'Oh, hello, darling,' said Penny, disguising her
attempted shift of tone with a little coughing fit. She
had been meaning to take a very preoccupied, Genius
at Work attitude to the call, but since it was from
Nicola she made an effort to sound pleased. Besides,
Nicola hadn't called her 'Mum' for years and Penny
felt a sharp tug on the old heartstrings.

'Listen, Mum, I'll cut to the chase,' said Nicola. 'I know we've had our differences in the past, but I just want to say that Nigel and I, and the children of course, although they don't know the details obviously, are really grateful for the "hot tip" you've given us on *wot u starin at*. We've bet all our savings on it and we're going to use the money to redo the roof, which is seriously needed – there's a huge stain in Lucy's ceiling and I wake in the middle of the night thinking the whole thing is going to collapse on her! Anyway, my point is, that I know it can't have been easy for you, being in a position of responsibility and everything, but as far as I'm concerned, it really helps to see you put family first.'

Penny had completely forgotten about the bet.

'You're welcome, darling,' she managed to blurt out, her mind swimming with the horrendous implications of Nicola's gratitude, as she put the phone back on the cradle.

She couldn't allow herself the luxury of dwelling on the bet. She pulled herself out of her trance, bustling about her flat, running a bath and laying out the dress she was planning to wear that evening. Worried as she had been about Nicola's call, it couldn't destroy the sense of ancient excitement that still clung to a rendezvous with David. He might be ninety-two (in fact he was ninety-two) but she could still feel the man behind the disintegrating human being. She would never forget the shock of being asked out by him for the first time and realizing that his interest in her was more than purely professional. Their first dinner took place during a long summer's evening at the end of the Falklands war, and David's comments had stayed with her ever since.

'I think this small war is a very good thing,' he said, looking out from the dining room of the Savoy Hotel onto the dark flood of the Thames, flecked with golden evening light. 'The young people of this country have had a taste of blood, and now they know what we went through during the War.'

The 'we' had particularly gratified her. He seemed to know instinctively that although she may not have been zigzagging across Normandy beaches under heavy enemy fire, or thundering through the streets of Berlin while SS suicide squadrons stuffed grenades down the muzzle of her Churchill tank, she had seen her favourite doll's house disappear in pretty hair-raising circumstances.

When David had touched her forearm, that first dinner, to emphasize a point he was making about the importance of Gibraltar remaining in British hands, she felt her body answer with a resounding Yes. It was the power of her boss, the recently knighted Permanent Secretary of the Foreign Office, of course, and of his brilliant intelligence, but it was also the power of a lonely and frustrated widower whose wife had died tragically the year before; above all, it was a power that would soon tear down the frail defences of her marriage and what she had imagined until then to be her moral code.

24

It was a long time since Sonny could remember being in such a good mood. John Elton had sent Auntie a letter of rejection that went far beyond the formal regret that usually characterized such documents and came sublimely close to insolence. On the other hand, his own persistent enquiries had revealed that *The Mulberry Elephant* was being treated with the greatest respect by IPG and had been passed on to a leading editor. To celebrate this delightful shift in relative prestige, Sonny was throwing a tea party in the Arnold Bennett Suite. He had got hold of his old acquaintance Didier Leroux and also left half a dozen unanswered messages for Katherine Burns.

What better time to give a literary tea party than during the announcement of the Elysian Short List? He would be the witness of Auntie's inevitable exclusion from the last stages of the competition, and at the same time surround himself with witnesses to his own innocent socializing at the moment when a fatal accident befell Malcolm Craig MP – if only he had got round to asking Mansur. Occurring only minutes after he announced the list of undeserving authors, his death would have struck the world as the very pattern of divine retribution. If the police became involved, Auntie and Didier would remember fondly being entertained by Sonny, not only with lashings of fruitcake but with favourite family anecdotes on literary topics, such as Somerset Maugham's visit to Badanpur, his famously acid remarks about his fellow guests, and his infatuation with one of the palace servants, whom he tried to press into his service, forcing the wretched fellow to beg Sonny's grandfather for protection from the great English story-teller!

Mansur, whose intelligence it was all too easy to question, but whose loyalty and propensity for violence could never be doubted, would follow his master's instructions slavishly, once he had been given them, steal a small unassuming car and run down the impudent chairman like a rabid dog. Without revealing his motives, Sonny had taken the precaution of sending Mansur to Oxford Street to buy a short zip-up jacket and a pair of common blue jeans. In London these days an embroidered frockcoat and a silk turban would not go unremarked, and since the escape plan consisted of Mansur melting into the crowd, the provision of a dreary modern costume was the least Sonny could do. The poor fool had turned up that morning in his new uniform, but still wearing a pair of beautiful Indian slippers. Sonny quite lost his temper, tossed him a small bundle of fifty-pound notes and ordered him to go and buy himself a pair of lime-green trainers! Mansur looked so crestfallen that Sonny actually apologized for scolding him. Truly, there was something magnificent about a man in Sonny's position humbling himself before a servant. Once he was alone again, staring dreamily over the roofs of Mayfair, picturing Mr Craig crushed against a bollard or a lamp-post, the thought of that exquisite courtesy had brought tears to his eyes and, in an act of further contrition, he went on to imagine Mansur slipping into the Underground and getting away without any unpleasant consequences.

Auntie was the first to arrive.

'What's that wireless doing in the middle of the

table?' she asked. 'I thought we were having a tea party.'

'Of course there will be tea and cakes,' said Sonny, 'but we will all be huddled around the wireless for the five o'clock broadcast of *Inkwell* on Radio Four. Don't touch the dials – they've already been set! Malcolm Craig will be announcing the Elysian Short List live from a press conference in Somerset House.'

'Oh, no,' said Auntie, 'I don't think my nerves could take it after that vile letter from Mr Elton. I told him it was a cookery book, but he simply wouldn't listen, and then . . .'

'Don't torture yourself by thinking about that letter,' said Sonny angrily. 'You can only do yourself harm by dwelling on those insults: "no trace of literature or any hint of imagination" – how dare he say such a thing? Hopefully, he will be proved wrong by this afternoon's broadcast.'

'Of course he won't,' said Auntie, clicking her tongue. 'Whoever made the mistake in the first place, there's no question of my little book being a finalist for the world's most famous fiction prize. It's really too ridiculous. I wish I hadn't been put on any list at all.'

'There, there,' said Sonny. 'You'll drive yourself mad by thinking about that letter.'

Auntie suddenly withdrew her attention. With her back straight, her hands folded in her lap and her gaze resting on a midpoint in the carpet, she seemed to have taken refuge in the heights of an invincible aloofness. Sonny grew nervous, feeling that he had gone too far with his patronizing reassurance.

After a few minutes, the painful silence was alleviated and amplified by the rattle of pots, jugs and plates, and the clink of heavy silver on a table wheeled in by the waiter to whose solicitous enquiries Sonny gave sullen and abrupt replies.

'Over there, over there . . . not that chair . . . don't bother, we'll help ourselves.'

When Didier eventually arrived, only ten minutes before the *Inkwell* broadcast, Auntie had still not surrendered to Sonny's offer of tea, and only gave a cold, vague greeting to his friend.

Sonny threw himself on Didier and started to describe Auntie's book in the most flattering terms, hoping to melt her resistance with an overheard eulogy.

'Of course, we're hoping to see *The Palace Cookbook* move from the Long List to the Short List in just a few minutes,' Sonny concluded, his hypocrisy made sincere by his panic-stricken desire to win Auntie back.

'Oh, honestly,' said Auntie, 'it's just a few recipes and some family portraits. There's been some sort of mistake . . .'

'Evidently,' said Didier, before Auntie could complete her self-deprecation, 'the intention of the author is not the measure of the text. We are not living in the nineteenth century! We are not going to sit here, even in the Arnold Bennett Suite, pretending that Roland Barthes never wrote *The Death of the Author*.'

'Perhaps we could take up that interesting point,' said Sonny, 'after the broadcast.' He leant over to switch on the radio.

'Oh, please,' said Auntie, restraining his hand, 'I really don't see the point.'

'Shhh,' said Sonny, 'we'll miss the beginning.'

'Frankly, I'd rather miss the whole thing,' said Auntie. 'You're just doing this to torment me.'

'Auntie! How could you say such a thing?'

'Oh, very well . . .' said Auntie.

By the time Sonny was allowed to switch on the radio, Malcolm was already nearing the end of his introductory remarks.

'As to the selection process, all I can say is that if we had been asked to draw up a list of the six *worst* books we'd read this year, our task would have been a great deal easier – believe me, there was no shortage of candidates for that prize! But, of course, what we were in fact asked to do was to make a list of the six *best* books of the year, and that is, without doubt, a far stiffer challenge. Rather than attempt to describe the critical framework of our decisions, or the forces that we have tried to hold in balance, I shall simply read out the Short List. The press are free to criticize our decisions, but there should be no doubt that they were made by a team of thoroughly responsible, highly intelligent and passionate readers.

> *The Frozen Torrent* by Sam Black
> *The Enigma Conundrum* by Tim Wentworth
> *All the World's a Stage* by Hermione Fade
> *wot u starin at* by Hugh Macdonald
> *The Palace Cookbook* by . . .'

Auntie's name was drowned out by a cry of astonishment emanating from the author herself.

'*Bravo*,' said Didier, '*et bravo pour Sam.*'

'Congratulations,' said Sonny, extorting a smile from his drooping features.

'And last but not least,' Malcolm concluded, '*The Greasy Pole* by Alistair Mackintosh.'

Sonny switched off the radio.

'I really don't understand,' said Auntie, clicking her tongue again, 'especially after that offensive letter from Mr Elton.'

'Evidently,' said Didier, 'we are in the presence of the text-as-textile, as the *fabric*-ation that weaves a dissimulating veil over its apparent subject, expressing the *excess* of figurative language over any assigned meaning or, more generally, the excessive force of the signifier over any signified that tries to contain it. A recipe from the *Palace Cookbook* is also a recipe from the *Anarchist Cookbook*! Precisely because language explodes with meanings that subvert our logocentric reading of the text, including the text we call "Reality".'

'There you go, Auntie,' said Sonny, as if he'd understood every word of Didier's impenetrable excitement, 'Didier has put it all in perspective for you.'

'I suppose so,' said Auntie, a little stiffly. She sighed and allowed her shoulders to relax; she liberated her hands from her lap, and seemed to be taking in the tonic of the good news.

'Thank you, Monsieur Leroux,' she went on, smiling graciously at Didier, 'thank you for explaining that to us.'

'*De rien*,' said Didier.

25

Sam sat at his desk, his middle finger dented by the pressure of the pen he was pressing against the almost blank page. A small ink stain had spread around the pen's eager nib. Above it, scrawled diagonally across the right-hand corner, was a list of words that failed to form a sentence but represented a kind of warm-up for the nauseating responsibility of writing one: 'not, neither, nor, nothing, less, without, and above all, no'.

This little doodle of negativity, like a cough before a speech, prepared Sam for the obligation of writing despite having nothing to say; indeed, the obligation to write only when he had nothing to say, since only then could a new insight emerge. Should he start with a declaration, or a description, a dialogue, or a comparison?

Declarations would buckle under the weight of their undeserved positivity and end their sentences as denials.

The only description worth having was a description of the gaze that produced the description in the first place.

Dialogue was just characters discussing the plot, but there were no characters, and there was no plot. Why not throw open some quotation marks and bring them both into being, by saying something, by saying anything at all?

The dent deepened, the stain spread.

Comparisons didn't bear thinking about. The ceaseless traffic of correspondences between one resemblance and another – eagle nebulae, star fruit, frog suits, foxgloves, rapier wit – generated a craving for The Thing Itself, but everybody knew, or else should know, that The Thing Itself was just another comparison, once it had been fished out of the ocean of silence by a linguistic net in which every word existed in relation to all other words. Even if it was decked in the mayoral chains of a Proper Name, a word depended on its position in a sentence as well as its history. Paris could famously turn up in Texas, and Boston could stay quietly in Lincolnshire; Byzantium and Constantinople were buried under the busy streets of Istanbul, while Leningrad was St Petersburg for the second time. 'A table' was a table, not the table, this table or that table; it depended on the words before and after it, just as the object it pointed to depended on its entirely metaphorical legs. The object was assembled into an illusory autonomy from bits of wood, glue and metal, while the word for it was assembled into an illusory stability out of grammatical and semantic relationships. Nothing was whole or complete. The universe was expanding as it decayed, and the language that described it, turning nouns into verbs and verbs into nouns, gentrifying slang, coining neologisms, importing foreign words, and dumping obsolete ones, was doing its best to keep up.

Sam dropped his pen on the desk. It was all too complicated. To say anything at all would be a mistake.

The truth was that he had decided to start a new novel for entirely psychological reasons: to protect himself against an unhealthy obsession with the fate of *The Frozen Torrent*. It was all very well having 'nothing to say' in the sense of having no preconceived set of ideas about the fate of his characters and the course of his plot, remaining open, discovering the truth of a situation in the course of exploring it, all of that; but it was no good really having nothing to say: being blank, blocked, lost.

He couldn't think how to begin a new novel precisely because he was already too preoccupied with the fate of the last one; the disease was too well established for the protection to work. He might as well give in to a fever of hope, dread, second-guessing and imaginary interviews, weird dreams and troubling symptoms.

He had been unable to escape the universal media derision for the Short List. It gave him both a sense of shame at his own inclusion and a guilty exhilaration at his increased chances of victory. He had tried not to read the press, but couldn't help noticing that *The Frozen Torrent* was the favourite at Ladbrokes.

Last night he had dreamt that the reward for winning the prize had been changed from the usual eighty thousand pounds to a night in bed with Katherine Burns. Alan and Didier had mysteriously made it on to the List, despite not having written any novels. Also among the finalists was Attila the Hun, who spoke a barking barbarian language in which Sam turned out to be fluent. A translation of their conversation appeared above the stage of the Banqueting Room, like surtitles at the opera. On the stage itself, and on huge screens around the room, the Short List was examined under a microscope by a team of experts in white coats. They bickered constantly and assaulted each other over the head with inflated pig's bladders. When the winner was finally announced, she turned out to be an exceptionally tall woman in a silver sequined dress who strode majestically across the room, climbed some steps up to a circular bed and engaged in a long, deep kiss with Katherine, to the uproarious delight of the dissolute, sweating guests who sat at tables made of giant water lilies. Bitterly disappointed, Attila burst into tears and had to be hugged and comforted by his motherly agent, who told him that *Die Christian Dog* was 'a timeless masterpiece' and that he'd been 'robbed'. 'It's my karma,' said Attila, who turned out to be a Hollywood actor, 'what goes around comes around.' 'You mustn't blame yourself,' said his agent, rubbing his back, 'don't blame yourself, sweetie, it's not your fault.'

Sam woke up from his dream with a pounding heart and an urgent desire to empty his bladder. Since his break with Katherine, he had been woken several times a night, trickling with sweat and convinced that he was about to die of a heart attack. He would lie in his damp T-shirt, breathing carefully and debating whether to take one of the beta-blockers his doctor had prescribed for performance anxiety. The horror was both persuasive and routine, without its familiarity blunting each night's uniquely convincing chest pains. The Short Listing of *The Frozen Torrent* had reinforced his panic, as well as adding a layer of ambivalence to it. Would it be good to win or not? Would it be clumsy and tactless to accept the prize after Katherine's unfortunate exclusion from the competition? Would she hate him for it? In any case, victory would mean a big speech; trunks of beta-blockers sent ahead to Melbourne, New York, Shanghai and Berlin; countless interviews using exactly the same formula to answer exactly the same question, and more and more photographs of him looking wooden and miserable. At the same time, it was out of the question not to win. And it was out of the question to have the thought that it was out of the question not to win. Hubris was bad, but insincere anti-hubris was no better. In the middle of the day, a word like 'humility' would present itself, like a sunlit colonnade in all its elegance and simplicity, but by the middle of the night it was transformed into a sinister ruin, with a murderer concealed behind every column.

Sam picked up his pen and wrote, 'In the middle of the day, a word like "humility" would present itself, like a sunlit colonnade in all its elegance and simplicity, but by the middle of the night it was transformed into a sinister ruin, with a murderer concealed behind every column.'

26

Vanessa opened *The Greasy Pole* with dutiful resignation. Knowing that it had passed onto the Short List with the support of all the other committee members assuaged her guilt at not having read it before. It had been selected through a series of mutually beneficial deals, rather than from any spontaneous enthusiasm. Jo, it was true, had said that it passed her 'relevance test' with 'flying colours', and Penny, rather obscurely, said that it was a relief to get a book that was 'actually *about* something', but other than that, Vanessa had no sense of its merits. Now she had to marshal arguments against it (assuming it turned out not to be a masterpiece) in order to secure victory for *The Frozen Torrent*, the only remaining work of literature on the list.

She cleared her mind and tried to read the text with as much receptiveness as possible.

As his train hurtled from Edinburgh to London, from capital to capital, Angus Stewart, the youngest Member of Parliament to be returned to Westminster after the closest election for a generation, felt a familiar pang of loss, and a no less familiar pang of anger, at leaving his fair homeland for the riot-torn nation to the south. London, Birmingham, Manchester, Salford, Nottingham, Liverpool, one after another the English cities had been ignited, filling the television screens of peaceful Scottish homes with images of destruction and chaos, and making Angus more determined than ever to break free from the cursed Union between his country and its bullying neighbour; a forced marriage between a comely maiden and a lustful old man, long overdue for dissolution, and too steeped in injustice to be remedied by any other means than divorce. One day, God willing, Angus would be the Prime Minister of a proud and independent Scotland, husbanding its own resources; its own oil, when the contracts with foreign petroleum companies came up for renewal, its own fisheries, once the quotas could be renegotiated with the EU, its own Toyota factories, and its very own wind farms.

Angus's deep clear eyes, like two Highland lochs, settled on the young man in sportswear sitting opposite him, and he felt a politician's instinctive desire to reach out to ordinary voters, and find out what they were thinking about the great issues of the day.

'So, what do you make of these English riots?' he asked with a broad smile.

'Well, I seen this policeman on TV last night,' said the young voter, 'and he said a gang is people that intimidates members of the public, right? So, I thought, in that case, the biggest gang out there is the police, right?'

'So would you be in favour of reforming their stop and search powers?' asked Angus.

'What I'm in favour of, mate,' said the young voter, 'is rioting. I want some of that free stuff I seen on TV . . .'

When Vanessa heard her phone ring she reached impatiently into her handbag to switch it off, but seeing that the call was from Penny, she decided to take it after all.

'Hello, Penny, how are you?'

'Well, I'm rather reeling from the news. Have you heard?'

'No.'

'Fasten your seat belt,' said Penny. 'It turns out that Malcolm's old boss at the Scottish Office is the author of *The Greasy Pole*. Alistair Mackintosh is just a pseudonym. Can you beat it? Malcolm has been quite subtly, not to say cunningly, pushing that novel in the hope of currying favour with a senior colleague.'

'What a coincidence, I was just about to read it,' said Vanessa, disguising the intensity of her disgust. 'It was the only one I hadn't got round to yet.'

'Oh, don't worry, we're all behind with our home-work,' said Penny. 'In his defence, I don't think Malcolm meant any harm. It was just a prank that went rather too far. And, as he says, there's nothing on record to show that he promoted the book himself.'

'Except in all our memories,' said Vanessa.

'Well, quite,' said Penny. 'He did persuade Tobias, and I'm afraid me, to vote it onto the Short List. Neither of us had the chance to have a *proper* look at it, but I suppose we just trusted him as Chairman.'

'So we're down to five books,' said Vanessa. And

we should be down to four judges, she thought. She wanted Malcolm to resign, she wanted him to be publicly reprimanded, but as she imagined the scandal unfolding, a certain world-weariness came over her. There seemed to be no one in a position of power, from the Vatican to Wall Street, from Parliament to Scotland Yard to Fleet Street, who could think of anything better to do than abuse it; besides, if Malcolm lost his authority, it might improve the chances for *The Frozen Torrent*.

'Yes' said Penny, 'one book each, which is fair. Mind you, I'm not fanatical about my choice. I'm prepared to concede gracefully if nobody else likes *Conundrum*.'

'Well, I'm sure we all think it's a ripping yarn,' said Vanessa, 'but perhaps it's not quite right for this prize.'

'That's probably true,' said Penny, 'in fact, we might as well say that we're down to four.'

Vanessa was struck by Penny's acquiescence, not to say her eagerness to get rid of her candidate, but she was too relieved to question it.

'I'll tell the others,' said Penny, 'to count *Conundrum* out.'

'If that's what you want,' said Vanessa, trying not

to sound as pleased as she felt. 'How's Malcolm taking it?'

'He's very robust,' said Penny, 'and unapologetic. Frankly, he seems more put out by discovering that the author of *wot u starin at* is not only a well-paid lecturer in medieval love poetry at Edinburgh University, but none other than The Mc Dougal of Mc Dougal, one of the most ancient titles in Scotland. It makes Malcolm's blood boil to think that he pretended to write a book of gritty social realism, when in fact he was leading a life of extreme privilege, dividing his time between his ancestral castle and a set of plush rooms in a prestigious university.'

'It doesn't really matter,' said Vanessa.

'Quite!' said Penny. 'It should be judged on its merits alone. Absolutely. Well, I'll see you at the next meeting. Down to four: we're really coming into the home straight.'

Vanessa switched off her phone, dropped it back in her bag and tossed *The Greasy Pole* onto the floor under the table.

She suddenly had a free afternoon. She could rush to meet her next responsibility and mark the first year's essays on Insanity and Alienation in Tennyson. All of them would quote, 'And my heart is a handful of dust' from *Maud*; most of them would quote the climax of grief from *In Memoriam*, 'And ghastly thro' the drizzling rain / On the bald street breaks the blank day'; some of them would get round to Tithonus's, 'Me only cruel immortality / Consumes', and point out how alienating it must have been to have his girlfriend turn him into a grasshopper; but most of all, the discussion would centre on that cautionary tale of opium addiction, *The Lotos-Eaters*, since most undergraduates knew little about alienation and insanity except from their self-imposed drug experiences.

On the other hand, she could leave her suddenly free afternoon free: she didn't have to cram it with new obligations, or move her schedule forward to annihilate the unexpected good fortune of a few uncluttered hours. She had read enough about Poppy's illness over the years to know that an anorexic's mother was typically a highly controlling perfectionist. Feeling the strain of leaving her afternoon empty, she made a concession to magical thinking and let herself believe that if she resisted imposing control on this stretch of free time she would be indirectly helping Poppy to recover.

It was a pity to ignore the thesis she was supervising, just when the semi-colon was about to reach its nineteenth-century peak of power and prestige; and difficult to neglect her own artful analysis of Undine Spragg's mother, which took the reader around Wharton's oeuvre, as well as fairly deep into the social history of her age: the rapidly changing attitudes to divorce, the high concentration of American fortunes in female hands, and so on and so forth; but these insights would have to wait. This afternoon, she would not let her judgemental mind characterize as mere laziness the subtle therapeutic space she was opening for her daughter. Just as an anorexic has to walk down the street rejecting the abundance of food offered on all sides, wasn't there something punitive and self-defeating about turning down an opportunity to stop working, to relax, to play? Wasn't there a family resemblance between the inability to take in nourishment and the inability to rest?

Queen Victoria's physician, Sir William Gull, who catalogued anorexia and gave it the surname 'Nervosa', was also suspected of being Jack the Ripper. An expert on treating nervous women, he may also have been an expert on making women nervous, occupying that disturbing border between the healer and the killer, where a surgeon's knife could be used to save a life or to end it. What good could come from a realm of mental illness claimed by such a sinister conquistador?

Even if there was some connection between Vanessa's need to rest and Poppy's need to eat, it was problematic for Vanessa to take the lead in doing nothing. Poppy would read Vanessa's inspiring example as a manipulative strategy, a covert attempt to rob her of control with the cheap sacrifice of an afternoon's work. Anorexia had been unknown in the Third World until the advent of Western television: it was supremely the disease of social comparison, of fatal competitiveness, of the final consummation of advertising, in which the image of emaciation is consumed rather than any product promoted by it.

Nevertheless, Vanessa decided that she would spend her afternoon without reading, or marking, or correcting, or writing. She would never tell Poppy, but she would just sit there thinking about her kindly, hoping it wasn't too late to stop being too busy.

27

Katherine was woken at two in the morning by a shock of shame.

What could she have been thinking of? John Elton; the dark green sofa in his hotel room; the coffee table pushed roughly aside; property magazines slithering clumsily to the carpet; his socks still on; her yearning to run through the door she could see reflected in the mirror above the fireplace, and her horrified sense, as the cluster of clinking glasses on the tray toasted her abasement, that she had found a new level of alienation in her erotic journey, something like volunteering to be raped.

After so many failures, was she smothering the possibility of a sane intimacy? Instead of waiting for love to turn into indifference or desire into disgust, why not embrace the disgust from the beginning, in an act of proleptic despair? Or was she just taking the logic of promiscuity to its absolutely indiscriminate conclusion?

She was back in her own bed now, without Elton, and yet her feeling of anxiety was growing stronger. John Elton was not an exotic object of desire; he was the antidote to desire. Once sex was a way to avoid affection, who better to choose? Only the catastrophe of an encounter with him could show just how vicious her resistance was. He was there to unveil the truth that she would rather fuck a man who repelled her than get close to one she really liked. Alan had been kind to her, in a rather fatherly way perhaps, but genuinely kind. Didier was an enthusiast. And Sam, well, Sam was in love with her and wanted to know her as deeply as possible, and that was why she had to get rid of him.

She would rather not get too close to anyone who might really understand her. Besides, Sam was a novelist. There was no room in the same bed for two people in the same business. And yet, if she was going to do this thing, Sam was the one to do it with. If she was going to challenge her paranoia, she might as well challenge her egoism as well. She suffered from as much ordinary selfishness as the next person, but piled on top of that she had the special affliction of a novelist, of wanting to be the author of her own fate and take charge of a narrative whose opening chapters had been written by others with terrifying carelessness. Her need to decide what things meant came no doubt from having lived so close to the sense that they meant nothing at all. At the very least she had to inhabit a world in which things never quite meant what they appeared to mean, where the margin of invention and interpretation was broader than it was, for instance, in the final moments of asphyxiation. Could she bear to have Sam nailing down the meaning of things with his own precision and his own perspective, or bear to see her interpretations seep into his work?

If only this latest ecstasy of shame and pointless sex would act on her with the chastening effect that an outstanding blackout sometimes has on an alcoholic. Waking in a strange place, looking back on an unqualified amnesia, with only bloodstained clothes for evidence; unsure whether the blood comes from a nosebleed or a murder (whose nosebleed? whose murder?), the drunk might think, as the corrosive dread colonizes every particle of her identity, 'I really must stop living this way.'

Fully awake now and knowing that sleep could not catch up with her racing mind, she got out of bed to make a cup of tea, but soon retreated from the hygienic brightness of the kitchen to the battered armchair where she often wrote, picking up a velvet cushion and pressing it to her lap. She stared out of her dark drawing room at the restless plane trees in the square, shaking sudden rushes of raindrops from their wet leaves, half shining in the lamplight and half heaving with shadow. She hadn't responded to any of Sam's emails since she stopped seeing him, but now she felt like getting back in touch. The simplest way, not too precipitous, and with the further benefit of disarming her competitiveness, would be to congratulate him on making the Elysian Short List.

She picked up the laptop from the small round table beside her and scrolled down to the last forlorn email from Sam, ignored its contents, clicked on *Reply* and wrote,

> *Congratulations*
> *Kx*

With a gambler's excitement at making an instantaneous and irreversible decision, she sent the email a moment later. She then felt rather depleted and impatient, wondering how long it would be before she would get a reply. It was only just after three in the morning. He probably wouldn't answer until lunchtime. She was about to close her glowing screen when a new item appeared in her inbox. It was from Sam.

> *Thanks.*
> *Do you want to come to the Elysian dinner with me?*
> *Sx*

Without hesitating she replied.

> *Love to.*
> *Kxx*

28

Penny ordered another Cosmopolitan from the waiter. She was having a thoroughly enjoyable time in no less a place than the Jardin Intérieur of the Paris Ritz. None of the other members of the committee had been able to come along on the trip and all she could say was 'more fool them'. With ten thousand euros entirely at her disposal, she had seen no reason not to take a suite at the Ritz for two nights, instead of the one night she had originally planned, go on a special guided tour of the Paris sewers, and book herself a table in the tip-top Michelin-starred restaurant conveniently situated in her own hotel. She had bought a vintage chart from her local wine merchant so as not to be bamboozled by a smooth-talking *sommelier* into paying through the nose for an inferior product.

Penny took a gulp of her second (absolutely delicious) Cosmopolitan and skewered a spicy green olive with a very smart white toothpick sporting a little black ribbon at one end. This really was perfection: getting a bit tipsy in these charming surroundings. You couldn't beat the French when it came to classical elegance. To her right was a white marble sphinx crouched on her leonine legs, with her hair up in a bun and a bow tie around her long neck. Other white marble statues of heroic male and modest female figures were dotted among the white paving stones of the garden and, at the end of the vista, high up on the far wall and seeming to preside over the whole space, was a medallion of an old man with a flowing beard; probably our friend Neptune, thought Penny, although the only water in the garden was hardly oceanic: it trickled from a fountain encased in a small white temple. Stone urns containing box, cut into perfect spheres, provided a few restrained green notes.

She had read in one of her guidebooks that the Ritz was a favourite haunt of Marcel Proust's. Although she sympathized with his choice of watering hole, Penny couldn't help reflecting that he was exactly the kind of author who would *not* have made it onto this year's Short List. She hadn't actually read any Proust, but she knew perfectly well that he was a long-winded snob, with far too much private money and some very unconventional sexual tastes: just the sort of thing they had been trying to avoid.

Apparently, Hemingway had also been a regular at the bar. She hadn't read Hemingway since doing *A Farewell to Arms* for O-level, but his manly, no-nonsense style, dealing with the great themes of love and war and the eternal puzzle of human nature, had given Penny's young imagination a strong sense of what real literature was all about. He would undoubtedly have fared better with the committee than the degenerate Proust. At least he had *done* something with his life other than go to parties and complain about his health. He was a man of action who had hunted big game, caught big fish and jumped on a plane the moment war broke out anywhere in the world, which of course kept him very busy during the nineteen-thirties.

Seeing that she had twenty minutes left before her table reservation in the restaurant down the corridor, Penny couldn't resist ordering another 'Cosy' as she had privately nicknamed what was rapidly becoming her favourite cocktail of all time.

'O-U-T spells OUT, so *out* you go,' Penny muttered under her breath, imagining the crestfallen, coughing Proust being forced to leave the magic circle of her table in the garden. It struck her as pretty historic – if that was the word – that one of the authors most celebrated for enjoying this splendid setting was being banished from the prestigious Short List by a member of the Elysian Prize committee, while she was relishing a drink in the very same spot!

It was all very well getting rid of Proust and sparing the plainspoken Hemingway, but what her committee had utterly failed to decide was which author was actually going to *win* this year. 'Win-wine / wine and dine', Penny invented a little ditty and sang it gently to herself.

She was just the teeniest bit tiddly and arguably should restrict herself to drinking wine by the glass over dinner. Mind you, it was rather a waste of the vintage chart to be stuck in the 'by the glass' section of a great wine list.

Where was she? Ah yes, the committee. It was in gridlock, rush-hour gridlock. The dinner was in three days, and nobody would budge. She and Malcolm were firmly committed to *wot u starin at*, with Jo and Tobias lined up against them, adamant about the virtues of the postmodern cookery novel. Vanessa was the floating voter who was driving them all mad, as she had from the word go. She was insisting that *The Frozen Torrent* was the only 'work of literature' on the List, and since there was no negotiation possible over the other two candidates, everyone should 'compromise' (i.e. cave in) and agree to her choice. Back in her Foreign Office days, Penny had naturally been involved in making her fair share of tough, unpopular decisions, but people had always known that she was acting from a sincere appraisal of the country's best interests – even if the country turned out to be Kuwait, or Saudi Arabia, or General Pinochet. Vanessa, by contrast, was being selfish for entirely selfish reasons. Penny was tempted to send her one of her famous letters – known at the Foreign Office as 'Penny's ICBMs' (Inter-Continental Ballistic Missiles). Although many of them, destined for an incompetent colleague, landed up in the same building from which they were sent, the 'Inter-Continental' tag gave you some idea of just how terrifying Penny could be when she got the wind up her.

'Arrogant bitch,' said Penny, just as the waiter arrived with her drink.

'Not you, of course,' she reassured the waiter.

'You're welcome, madame,' said the waiter in a
perfect German accent, bowing gravely as he placed
the cocktail in front of her. It was all tremendously
international, even at the staff level. She could hear
Russian being spoken by the entrance to the indoor
bar; there were Americans by the fountain, and there
was a Chinese man smoking a cigar further away,
next to a marble nymph trying to hide her private
parts. The French must be lurking somewhere, and
with Penny representing Great Britain, they could
have a Security Council meeting at the drop of a hat.

Penny took a sip of her new drink and looked up
at the side of the magnificent building next door. It
was nothing less than the French Ministry of Justice.
On arrival, she had been tremendously inspired to
find that her hotel shared a garden wall with such an
important civil service department. All she had ever
really wanted the prize to achieve was justice, and
now it felt like destiny to be sleeping on the eve of
the final meeting in a room that overlooked the very
pleasant gardens of a place that symbolized that ideal.

Penny closed her eyes and imagined herself as the
figure of Justice on top of the Old Bailey, blindfolded
and holding up a pair of scales in which she weighed
with absolute impartiality the endless pile of books

that had been sent to the committee. She hadn't cheated and taken a secret peek, although she had *listened* to some of the books. Nothing wrong with that: nobody had ever suggested that Justice should wear earplugs as well as a blindfold. At that rate, you might as well have her in a coma on a life-support machine!

No, Penny had done her best to embody Justice, but it had been complicated and, above all, exhausting and time-consuming. When she opened her eyes again, she found that her vision was already blurred and a moment later, as she melted into a full realization of what a strain it had all been, tears started to spill from her eyes. She picked up the little folded linen napkin from the table and dabbed her wet cheeks. To her horror, the German waiter was approaching at the very moment she didn't want to be seen by anyone.

'I probably look an absolute fright with all my make up running,' she blurted out as he arrived.

'You're most welcome, madame,' he said agreeably. 'Your table is ready, if you wish to proceed to the dining room. I will bring your cocktail.'

'Oh, don't worry about that,' said Penny, draining the conical glass.

It was time for a bit of the old *cuisine gastronomique*. She hoisted herself up, wandered back through the red bar and down the long blue corridor. French flag, she thought: white garden, red bar, blue corridor. She muttered encouragement to herself over the swish of her evening dress. After all, it wasn't every day that one found oneself enjoying Versailles levels of unabashed French luxury, with the welcome addition of modern plumbing.

In the Eurostar on the way over she had been mugging up on *The City Under the City* in her guidebook, and been reminded that Victor Hugo had set a very dramatic scene of *Les Misérables* in the Paris sewers. Without wishing to be a copycat, she thought she might do exactly the same thing and set a very dramatic scene of *Roger and Out* in that cloacal maze.

To be perfectly honest the sewers had been something of a disappointment, despite the VIP treatment, which had taken her far beyond the gift shop and educational displays set up for ordinary tourists. She had been given a pair of very serious gumboots, a waterproof boiler suit and a gas mask and then been guided by top experts deep into the vaulted tunnels. She trod along narrow pavements running beside swift torrents of wastewater. She crossed metal bridges over stagnant pools full of leaves and plastic bottles, cigarette butts, and other floating objects from the gutters above. She saw the gleaming tails of rats disappearing into narrower tunnels, or washing themselves, as bold as brass, under showers of effluent. All the tunnels were named after the streets above them, with exactly the same famous blue and white street signs. At first it was rather delightful to find oneself underneath the Quai d'Orsay, the famous address which was also the nickname for the French Foreign Office. Her teeming imagination couldn't help thinking that the sewers would be an excellent method for smuggling sensitive information out of the French F.O. without needing to be compromised by carrying it out oneself. Electronically tagged containers could be flushed down to agents waiting below (mental note: possible scene in *R and O*). She had passed under the Louvre with a frisson of secret pleasure, thinking of the huge queues trying to get into the museum, little suspecting that she and her guides had already gained access without the trouble of buying a ticket.

As they worked their way back in a wide arc, under the Tuileries Gardens and to the Place Vendôme,

Marcel, the chief guide, pointed out that her hotel suite was a couple of dozen metres above her head. She couldn't help having a little pang of longing for its charming garden views, its deliciously soft sheets and, at the other end of all this plumbing, the marble bathroom with its powerful shower and the sumptuous pink dressing gown hanging from a hook on the back of the door. She pressed on, though, down the rue du Faubourg St-Honoré, taking a keen interest in Marcel's description of the *boules de curage*: giant wooden spheres, only slightly narrower than the tunnels they were rolled through, that forced all the grit and waste into the main drain. She daydreamed about having a very powerful hose and a good old *boule de curage*, with Vanessa and Jo and Tobias on the other side of it, sprinting towards a swelling flood of sewage. All they would have to shout out to make the nightmare stop was '*wot u starin at*' and she would turn off the hose and set them free with a minimum of legal formality. Despite this enlivening fantasy, Penny started to grow a little weary of the tunnels, and when Marcel came to a halt and saluted facetiously, pointing his finger upwards and saying, 'Ambassade Britannique,' Penny felt a stab of nostalgia, remembering the old days when

David had once taken her to lunch at our splendid Paris embassy.

At that point, something in her rebelled and, as she struggled back to her starting point at the Pont de l'Alma, she allowed herself to reflect that on a visit to a great city whose dazzling architecture was infused with the spirit of all the art and music and literature that had been made there, and was still being made there, it was important not to set one's sights too low and end up labouring through a labyrinth of dark tunnels, up to one's knees in rivers of shit.

29

Alan put down *The Mulberry Elephant* with a puzzled frown. As always he had looked at the last page number before reading the first word. There were two thousand more pages of this stuff. At first, he couldn't quite believe that he wasn't being tricked, and that the Prince wouldn't turn out to be framed, or undermined in some way, but after skipping forward to several random passages later in the book, he confirmed that it was written entirely from the Prince's point of view, with a wearisome emphasis on the insults dealt by modernity to the glory of the princely states, and without any hint of relief from his cloying self-regard. It was a curious object, but clearly unpublishable.

Alan left the book behind to keep a claim on his table, and then joined the queue for tea and coffee, sliding his tray towards the cash register while he put in his order for another cappuccino. He had walked across Hampstead Heath to Kenwood House with *The Mulberry Elephant* pulling on the straps of his rucksack. The exercise, and the long enlivening light of midsummer, had reinforced the good mood brought on by James Miller's early call saying that IPG had decided to offer him a job. His reports on the other two typescripts had been 'exemplary' and the agency would be delighted to have such a senior editor on board. To celebrate the decision, he was invited to join the IPG table at the Elysian Prize dinner. Alan put down the phone with the feeling that he was back at the centre of literary life. Wanting to get shot of *The Mulberry Elephant* before returning to an office routine, but unable to stand the confines of his hotel any longer, he hit on the idea of spending the day in Hampstead, walking and working. Now, in less than an hour, his work was over. He had the rest of the day to himself – not the rest of his life, as he had imagined during those drunken weeks confined to his fetid hotel room, but the rest of his day, delicious because it was limited and precise.

He might not be living in the Mount Royal for the rest of his life either. Relations with his wife had taken on a more conciliatory tone. It was not his repentant emails nor her harsh replies that improved the atmosphere. It was the terrible innocence of his subsequent silence that won her over. He didn't break off contact with her as a tactic but from pure incapacity. Even when she was trying to hate him, Marilyn couldn't stop worrying about him. It was easy to reject his apologies but impossible to lose an interest in his whereabouts. Eventually the stronger species of emotion became entirely dominant, and Marilyn was worrying what state their marriage must have been in for Alan to defect, worrying about whether they could put the whole thing behind them, and worrying about Alan wasting money in hotels. Alan hoped that he would soon get an invitation back home but he knew that any pressure from him would delay its arrival.

The pain of his separation from Katherine, the sense that he had known something perfect and then lost it for ever, was a general numbing fact, like the strange quiet of a city early in the morning after a heavy fall of snow, but within it he could also hear, at unpredictable intervals, the hiss and the thud of a guillotine as certain details returned to his memory – the way, for instance, she had draped her arms around his neck and closed her eyes and stood a little on tiptoe to kiss him for the first time, making his enthralment look like her submission. When these images returned he had to pause if he was walking, sit down if he was standing, lie down if he was sitting, close his eyes if he was lying down, and stop breathing at all times, while he groped to deal with the fact that a fragment of his past was so much more immediate than the vaporous and destitute quality of his surroundings.

Three days ago, to his amazement, he had received a handwritten letter from Katherine. Recognizing the handwriting, he also recognized how ready he was to go back to her under any conditions; he imagined, with some embarrassment but without any doubt, the collapse of his reconciliation with Marilyn. He could have denied these impulses, since they only lasted for the few seconds between knowing that Katherine had written to him and finding out what she had written.

Dear Alan,

it began with unpromising formality.

> *I am writing to apologize for the mess*
> *I've made of things over the last year,*
> *luring you away from Marilyn and then*

dropping you so abruptly last month. You
gave me an excuse with the fuck-up over
Consequences, but I would have done it
anyway. I know how to make men fall in
love with me but then I don't know what
to do afterwards. That, along with my
infidelities, completes the picture of what
must seem to you a vile moral character.

That last sentence struck Alan as a false note. The
use of two clichés in a row showed that Katherine's
conviction was faltering: the 'complete picture' must
include many more faults than the two she was
owning up to and, since she knew that he was still
in love with her, it was a hidden request for him to
reject the Victorian charge of 'a vile moral character'
and overlook the very things she appeared to be
underlining.

I have come to a sort of crisis about all
of this, but all I can do right now is try to
stop creating chaos around me, and to ask
the forgiveness of the people I've obviously
wronged, most of all you.
Lots of love,
K

'Lots of love' between former lovers was of course less love than 'love' alone. Nevertheless, he was grateful that she had not asked him to lay waste to his life a second time, knowing how eagerly he would have complied.

Back at his table, Alan took a cautious sip of his cappuccino. The letter had been salutary; there was no doubt about that. It had broken the spell of Katherine as an inaccessible object of desire on which any amount of frustration and fantasy could be expended and replaced it with a struggling human being, lost and remorseful. Its disappointing contents had helped to wash away the last traces of his romantic folly. He had always been too frightened and self-preserving to fall madly in love in adolescence, or in his twenties, and when he was finally ready to take the risk, it had all gone terribly wrong, but that, after all, was the point of romantic folly. If it hadn't all gone terribly wrong, it wouldn't have been the real thing. Still, it was wonderful to have got that behind him. He drained his cup of coffee and got up decisively, as if he had settled something once and for all.

Fighting his desire to leave *The Mulberry Elephant* behind in the cafe, he loaded the enormous volume back into his rucksack, and set off with a sense of sober elation. He walked through the gate towards the Highgate side of the Heath, and down the sloping meadow to the fountain at the foot of the hill. He scooped a few handfuls of the cold iron-rich water into his mouth, amazed by the orange streaks that stained the mud where the fountain overflowed the encrusted drain. Their screens of thick foliage made him feel he was eavesdropping on the murmuring and splashing pleasures of the bathing ponds. He turned right and cut across towards Hampstead. As he strolled down the long avenue of limes that leads to East Heath Road, his path was crossed by a dog walker, surrounded by a scattered gang of at least twenty dogs weaving their way contentedly through the woods up to the Viaduct Pond.

Alan wanted to go to one of the nearby book-shops to buy something good to read on the way home, to rinse away the poisonous, syrupy taste of *The Mulberry Elephant* and remind him what literature was before he went to the Elysian Prize dinner the next night.

30

Penny was prepared to bet that the Fishmongers' Hall had never looked more magnificent. It had been especially re-decorated for the occasion, using black, in honour of the Elysian Group, and gold, in honour of their lucrative prize. The tablecloths were black and the candlesticks gold, the chairs were gold and the stage draped with immense black curtains, pelmets and swags. A gold podium stood in the centre with powerful television lights on either side, waiting to be switched on for the broadcast of Malcolm's announcement. It was what she felt like calling 'quite something'.

Downstairs, the other guests were arriving: writers, publishers, agents, journalists and so forth, but they would not be allowed into the Banqueting Room for another three-quarters of an hour. She wanted to drink it all in, knowing that she had the room to herself for the last time. The guests would mill about the State Drawing Room, drinking champagne, gawping at the royal portraits, and studying the seating plan displayed on an easel by the door.

Penny was of course on table No. 1, with the rest of the committee, nearest the stage. She wandered over to make sure that she was sitting next to her special guest, David Hampshire. On her other side was Liu Ping Wo, Chairman of Shanghai Global Assets, the new owners of the Elysian Group. How proud they must be to have taken over the prize and find themselves in one fell swoop at the very heart of British cultural life. Mrs Wo was on David's other side, and would no doubt be amazed by his detailed knowledge of the Chinese scene. David being David, he would probably keep his perfect Mandarin for dessert. She longed to see Mrs Wo's face when she realized that she was sitting next to a man who had translated some of Gladstone's famously long and complicated Budget speeches into Chinese as a pure intellectual exercise.

Penny looked through the tall windows at the swift flood of the Thames, racing under the arches of London Bridge while the city's myriad lights sketched a thousand white and orange doodles on its liquid surface. Then she looked back at the podium where the announcement of the winner was due to be made in three hours' time. What nobody outside the committee could have guessed was that its 'final' meeting had been far from conclusive. While London's literati were speculating wildly about this year's winner in the State Drawing Room, the committee was doing exactly the same in the Library. At this very moment Malcolm and Jo were engaged in desperate last-minute negotiations with Vanessa, fighting to secure her pivotal vote. Tobias had gone downstairs to 'check out the canapés', and Penny, unable to stand the tension, had chosen a moment of quiet reflection in the Banqueting Room.

When Auntie was invited to the Elysian dinner, she had replied saying that she would be bringing Monsieur Didier Leroux as her guest, and that she would also like to bring her publisher and her literary agent. These were the titles she was assigning to Sonny and Mansur in order to smuggle them into the Fishmongers' Hall. Auntie forgave herself this little white lie, knowing that every other Short-Listed author would

take for granted the sort of entourage she had con-
jured up by these dishonest means. Mansur had been
thrown into crisis by the prospect of sitting down to
dinner with his semi-divine employers, but Sonny,
who was usually rather a stickler in matters of rank,
surprised Auntie by insisting that Mansur come along.

'Don't be such an old stick in the mud,' said Sonny,
as their car drew up outside. 'Mansur is really one of
the family.'

Auntie's nightwatchman, gratified to the point of
panic, sat motionless in the passenger seat next to the
driver.

Auntie disguised her annoyance with Sonny by
opening her evening bag and checking for the tenth
time that it contained the acceptance speech Didier
had written for her. She hardly expected to win,
but the very obliging Monsieur Leroux had written
something for her, just in case.

Sam lay in Katherine's bed, in a pool of half-formed
dreams, not quite asleep, nor quite awake, his arm
wrapped loosely around her waist. For their reunion,
Katherine had taken him to a Japanese restaurant
for lunch. They drank a bottle of sake to celebrate

his Short Listing. It had made him think of spring rain and forests of swaying bamboo. When he leant against Katherine he felt their bloodstreams merging into a single flow. Back at her flat, they fell into bed and made love. He noticed that it was about four o'clock when she fished a small joint out of the drawer of her bedside table.

'I don't think I should,' he said

'Don't worry, it's not skunk, just some very friendly home-grown.'

When they made love again, everything was slower, as if the sensual freight had grown so heavy that time couldn't be expected to rush along as it used to. Afterwards, they fell into a kind of buzzing stillness, their breaths synchronized and their bodies moulded together.

'Christ! It's six-thirty,' said Katherine.

'Fuck,' said Sam, 'I've got to have a shower.'

'Together,' said Katherine, kissing him, calming him down and making him wonder if he wanted to leave at all.

John Elton arrived at the Fishmongers' Hall accompanied by Amanda, his irresistible assistant. He did something much more thrilling than sleep with Amanda: he made people think he was sleeping with her. When they were out together, the only restriction he put on her conversation was any mention of her boyfriend, or any explicit denial that she was having an affair with her boss. She generally said, 'John and I are very close,' or, 'That's for you to wonder,' or, 'Mind your own business,' depending on how late it was and how many times she had been asked. She was paid a bonus for her evening work and, as she explained to her friends, 'It's like being an escort without the sex – pretty ideal really.'

John was the agent for *All the World's a Stage*. The author, Hermione Fade, had refused to fly in from Christchurch, New Zealand, unless she was told that she going to win. John pleaded with the Elysian Group for a little advanced notice, but received a very stony reply from David Hampshire, saying that it was 'out of the question to give any hints of any sort whatever about the outcome of the prize'. John was authorized to deliver a speech on Hermione's behalf if *All the World's a Stage* won. He had it tucked in his inside pocket; it was a theatrically confident manifesto for historical fiction perfectly crafted for the confident theatrical historical novel it celebrated.

The sight of Auntie and Sonny, standing under a larger than life portrait of the portly, blue-sashed George IV in a bright red coat and white wig, spoilt John's proprietary sweep into the State Drawing Room. Despite his contempt for *The Palace Cookbook*, he couldn't help reproaching himself for a lack of cynicism: to have two books on the Short List, especially one that was so ludicrously unworthy, would have done his reputation for shrewdness and prescience no harm. 'Sometimes you have to read the judges rather than the books,' he could imagine himself saying in the long *Vanity Fair* profile that would one day inevitably be written about him.

By the time Alan arrived, the party had really kicked off: photographers were taking photographs of people they had photographed before, the quails' eggs had run out and one or two people were already quite drunk. Alan couldn't immediately see James Miller but was in no particular hurry to find him.

He had been over to Marilyn's to collect his dinner jacket and had ended up dressing in his old bedroom, finding his shaving foam and razor at the back of the cupboard under his basin, and his cufflinks in the little box in the drawer of his bedside table. After nearly a year of exile, he was taken over by a deeply familiar feeling of being at home, preparing to go out for the evening. Marilyn suggested that he move in over the weekend 'as an experiment'. He left Belsize Park with a sense of gratitude and security only slightly shadowed by loss and defeat.

In the taxi, he toyed with the wistful thought that he might have been going to the Elysian dinner with Katherine, that she might turn out to have won the prize and that they might return to her flat for a night of passionate celebration. As he approached his destination, he tried to chastise himself, but like a man who slaps the mosquito on his arm and then sees, as he withdraws his hand, that the crushed insect has already drawn blood, Alan realized that his intellect had arrived too late to stop his imagination from getting lost in an alternative reality that contained no reality at all.

As if to point out, from another angle, the futility of his attempted discipline, the first person to greet him was Yuri, his old employer at Page and Turner.

'Ah, Alan,' he said, with the brutal directness that he usually farmed out to his wife but was capable of reclaiming for special occasions, 'I suppose Katherine

would have been here if it wasn't for your inepti-
tude.'

Alan was too startled to think of a reply.

'I hear she has also given you the sack,' Yuri went
on. 'Everywhere I go I start a fashion!'

He gave Alan a blast of genial laughter, and then
turned away and started to stroll around the room,
dispensing charm.

Alan wandered over to the bar to give himself
time to recover. He dithered over what to drink, torn
between a cautious elderflower cordial and a consol-
ing glass of Jack Daniel's. Before he could make a
decision, he felt a hand on his shoulder.

'*Salut*, Alain!'

'Didier! What are you doing here?'

'So, this is the epicentre of English Literature,'
said Didier, smiling at Alan, 'located in the home of
a very successful fishmonger, under the gaze of dead
monarchs, in the narrow space between the hostility
of a philistine commerce and the indifference of a
philistine ruling class! Bravo for the artist who
survives in this environment! In France, it is the
opposite: everything is culture. It is a kind of nightmare. You walk down a street named after Voltaire,
your steak has apparently been cooked for Rossini,

and Chagal has designed the label on your bottle of wine. You rush to the country to escape the cultural density of the city, but the little waves lapping on the lakeshore belong to Rousseau and the birds that appear to be singing in the woods are in fact singing in a poem by Chateaubriand. Even a field of wheat is a cultural object, oppressed by its semiotic potential to become the world's most iconic loaf: the baguette!'

'Yes, but what are you doing here?' Alan persisted.

'I am the speech writer for one of the Small-Listed authors,' said Didier, hardly able to contain his mirth. 'My friend Sonny Badanpur has asked me to help his aunt . . .'

'Badanpur . . .' said Alan, 'has he written a very long novel?'

'Absolutely: *The Mulberry Elephant.* You have read it?'

'Yes, well, not all of it – it's twice the size of *War and Peace.* Which one is he? I must make sure I don't meet him; I just wrote rather a harsh report on his book.'

'By the fireplace with the yellow slippers,' said Didier. 'Ah,' he went on, looking over Alan's shoulder and suddenly growing animated, 'here is someone I'm sure you will want to see.'

Alan turned round, already knowing from Didier's tone what to expect. Framed in the doorway, her hair still tangled, and her mouth swollen by round after round of kissing and biting, stood Katherine, dishevelled enough to remind him that her beauty did not depend on what she was wearing. Next to her was Sam, looking sleepy and electrified at the same time; with his bowtie tilted, like an old-fashioned plane propeller that needed to be pulled down to get it started.

Before Alan could fully appreciate the rush of nausea and jealousy that passed through him, a tall man with white hair and a red tail coat, who might have stepped out of one of the mediocre portraits that encumbered the walls of the State Drawing Room, appeared at Katherine's side and started shouting slowly at the top of his voice.

'Your Excellencies, my Lords, Ladies and Gentlemen! Dinner is served! Will you please proceed to the Banqueting Room.'

Here comes the human stampede, thought Penny, as she returned along the upper gallery, somewhat anxiously, after a fruitless search for the rest of the committee. They must have gone downstairs for a drink without bothering to let her know. Frankly, it defied belief, even if relations had become somewhat strained. Nevertheless, she must keep calm, park herself at table No. 1 and wait for the committee to come to her. Malcolm was sitting the other side of Mrs Wo from David, and so he was bound to turn up soon. The thought of David stopped Penny in her tracks. He could hardly be expected to make it up the stairs on his own. Why did she have to think of everything? The smart young women in black evening dresses, checking the guest list by the front door, would have simply ticked his name off the list and left him to fend for himself.

As the first guests arrived at the top of the stairs, Penny went in the opposite direction along the upper gallery to the small lift in the far corner of the building.

After confirming that he had arrived, she found David sitting in a gilt chair next to the Drawing Room doors, looking somewhat forlorn, with two walking sticks resting against the wall beside him.

'David!'

'Ah, Penelope, thank goodness you're here, I'm not sure I can manage these stairs.'

'Don't worry, I've thought of that,' said Penny, 'we have a lift specially prepared for you.'

David followed her painfully across the hall, with Penny saying, 'Take your time,' every five seconds.

'I am taking my time,' said David. 'I'm sorry it's so fucking slow, if that's what you're driving at.'

'No, I . . .' Penny was lost for words. There had always been a prickly side to David, but at this stage of their relationship, she really didn't appreciate having her head bitten off.

Before Penny could decide what to make of David's rudeness, she heard her name being called.

'Ah, Penny, there you are!' said Malcolm. 'David, good to see you! I'm afraid we've got rather a situation on our hands. Vanessa can't be persuaded to choose either of the finalists. She simply won't budge. The only other way is for one of us to change our minds. I wonder if you could track down Tobias and see if he's prepared to save the day by voting for *wot u starin at*.'

'I was going to take David up in the lift,' said Penny, who couldn't help marvelling at the way Malcolm had bounced back after the *Greasy Pole* incident.

'I'll do that,' said Malcolm, 'I need to have a word

with him about precedents. Could the prize be awarded jointly if we can't break this gridlock?'

'There is a precedent for that: 1978,' said David immediately, 'but it won't be popular with the Elysian board. They like a clear victor.'

'Well, I'd better hunt down Tobias and appeal to his team spirit,' said Penny. 'See you upstairs.'

Malcolm eventually managed to get inside the small panelled lift with David, and push the button for the first floor.

'You'll be sitting next to Mrs Wo,' he said. 'She's the wife of the man whose corporation has taken over the Elysian Group.'

'Bloody Chinks – they're taking over everything,' said David.

'Well, I'm sure you won't be putting it quite like that,' Malcolm hesitated as the lift jerked to a halt without the doors opening.

'Oh, you can't stop me now,' said David. 'It's the privilege of old age: I can speak my mind at last, after a lifetime of diplomatic toadying.'

Malcolm pressed the first-floor button several times to no effect. Although the news that David was renouncing his legendary charm and was planning to make a xenophobic attack on the evening's most important guests would normally have alarmed him, it hardly had any impact thanks to the spasm of anxiety he felt at the prospect of being trapped in a broken lift. He pressed the ground-floor button, and the second-floor button without getting any response.

'Are we stuck?' asked David.

'I'm afraid it looks that way.'

'Don't panic,' shouted David, swinging one of his walking sticks against the thudding metal doors with surprising violence. 'I have to tell you that I suffer quite badly from claustrophobia.'

'Please calm down,' said Malcolm firmly. 'We have an emergency telephone, and we'll soon have everything under control.'

'Don't panic!' shouted David a second time, poking his other stick at the ceiling and smashing one of the light bulbs.

Sam and Katherine arrived early at their table and quickly changed the place cards so as to be together. They stroked each other's thighs under the table, sometimes dreamily, sometimes fervently, unconcerned with the world around them, or so they thought, until a very agitated woman came and sat down next to Sam.

'I'm sorry to interrupt you,' she said, 'but I feel that there's something I must tell you.'

'Oh, hi,' said Sam. 'You are?'

'Sorry, I'm Vanessa Shaw. I'm one of this year's judges, and I really wanted to apologize to you personally.'

'What? You voted against *The Frozen Torrent*?'

'No, no, I voted for it.'

'I forgive you,' said Sam. 'We forgive her, don't we?' he said to Katherine.

'Yeah, you're forgiven,' said Katherine, smiling, while her nails grazed the hollow behind Sam's knee.

'No, you don't seem to understand,' said Vanessa. 'I wasn't able to get your book through. It was by far the best piece of writing; in fact it was the only book of any literary merit at all. I'm really sorry – you should have won.'

Vanessa's voice faded; a film of tears formed over her dark blue eyes.

'You probably shouldn't be telling me this, should you?' said Sam.

'I'm sorry, of course you're right,' said Vanessa. 'I was afraid I would miss you after the announcement, and I wanted you to know how passionately I feel about your book and what a terrible injustice it is. The only consolation I can offer is that *The Frozen Torrent* will last; it'll be read long after all the other books on this list have been forgotten.'

'We don't know that yet,' said Sam. 'Time grinds everything to dust, but one or two things are hard enough to dent the millstones and fall through intact – on the first round.'

Sam picked up the menu of that evening's dinner, as if to distract himself from this astral perspective of human affairs. He ran his eyes over the delights in store.

'By the way, do you know Katherine Burns?' he asked.

'Oh, hello,' said Vanessa, 'pleased to meet you. I'm a great admirer of your work. Do you have a novel coming out soon?'

'Next week,' said Katherine.

'But why wasn't it submitted to us?'

'Oh,' said Katherine, wondering how much detail to go into, and finally opting for opaque simplicity, 'they fucked up.'

'I can't exactly thank you for what you've told me,' said Sam, 'but it may save us the trouble of working our way through the goat's cheese, beetroot and salmon mousse.'

He turned to Katherine, pressing his palm gently but emphatically against her lower back. 'Shall we go, or shall we stay?' he asked.

Tobias gave an ingratiating smile to Mr and Mrs Wo, who were looking with what he took to be solemn displeasure at the empty chairs which should have been occupied, according to their stiff little place cards, by The Right Honourable Malcolm Craig, MP, Sir David Hampshire and Miss Penny Feathers.

'I'm afraid we will have to start without the Chairman,' said Mr Wo. 'We're on a tight schedule with the television broadcast.'

Tobias sat down uneasily next to Mrs Wo, wondering where on earth the committee had fled to. He imagined himself having to improvise a speech about the importance of literature, the encouragement of new talent, the generosity of Shanghai Global Assets and, last but not least, the insufferable drabness of his fellow judges. Instead of a dinner jacket – the world's dreariest uniform, which he would only consent to wear if he were asked to star in a West End production of a play about an eloquent head waiter – Tobias was wearing a black velvet frock coat, a double-breasted dark grey waistcoat, and a dark purple silk tie with a pearl pin. There was no doubt he looked good tonight. Not only that, but he had once memorized Shelley's *Defense of Poetry* to impress his English teacher in a talent competition at school, so as to get the lead part in that summer's production of *Hamlet*. The key bits about poets being the unacknowledged legislators of the world had stayed with him and would make an impressive introduction to the section on the importance of literature. There was also a striking phrase of Shelley's, which had been a particular favourite of his English teacher's, about 'imagining that which we know'. He must try to work it in somewhere. As to the radical originality of this year's winner, it would help to know which book he would be attributing that quality to.

'Red or white?' asked the waiter, rousing Tobias from his private thoughts.

'Do you think you could lay your hands on a bottle of whisky?' Tobias asked. 'I'm allergic to wine, you see.' He generally found a fake allergy was taken more seriously than a simple request.

'I'll see what I can do, sir.'

'You could just bring us the bottle. I'm sure Mr Wo would like a drop.'

'My husband is a teetotaller,' said Mrs Wo, putting her phone back into her evening bag.

'Oh, well, I'll have to dispatch it all on my own,' said Tobias, with an amusingly martyred sigh. 'If it were done when 'tis done, then 'twere well / It were done quickly.' Seeing that Mrs Wo was not especially amused by his allusion to the Scottish play, he switched smoothly to a tone of great seriousness.

'So, are you a keen reader yourself, Mrs Wo? Forgive me, I really ought to know, but is it pronounced "wo" or "woo"?'

"Wo – as in "woe is me", something I can truly say,' laughed Mrs Wo. 'But to answer your question, Mr Benedict, I am reading Virginia Woolf's notebooks at the moment; so fresh, with all the visual brilliance of the novels, but much more relaxed and natural. You agree?'

'I worship the notebooks,' said Tobias. 'I was once asked to play Leonard Woolf in a film that never got made, but I devoured the notebooks for weeks.'

'In China we put great emphasis on this naturalness, which of course can only come from the mastery of artifice.'

'I can see you've been into these questions very deeply,' said Tobias, twisting around to see if his whisky was on its way yet. He had snorted a couple of lines of coke in the loo and really needed to take the edge off. What he saw instead of the waiter was Sam Black, whom he recognized from the photograph on the dust jacket of *The Frozen Torrent*, weaving his way towards the door, with an extremely attractive woman close behind him. There was something definitive about their way of leaving.

'They flee from me that sometime did me seek,' he muttered to himself.

'I'm sorry?' said Mrs Wo.

'Oh, I was just struggling to remember a quotation – about naturalness and so forth.'

'Ah, there are so many!' said Mrs Wo. 'Picasso saying he could draw like Raphael when he was a child but it took him his whole life to learn how to draw like a child; or La Rochefoucauld . . .'

'Ah, La Rochefoucauld,' said Tobias, delighted at the discovery of a mutual friend.

'Thank you,' said Mrs Wo unexpectedly, inviting Tobias to turn around.

Standing behind them was a muscular young man

in a black suit, holding a bottle of Johnny Walker Blue Label.

'When I heard you asking for whisky I texted my driver; we always keep a bottle in the car, in case one of our friends would like a "wee dram",' said Mrs Wo, giggling at her imitation of a Scottish accent.

'That's more than generous of you,' said Tobias, in a Scottish accent of his own. 'I must say, Mrs Wo, you're a woman full of surprises! Let's drink a toast to naturalness: art's greatest achievement!'

'With pleasure,' said Mrs Wo.

Sonny was thoroughly disconcerted by Malcolm's absence and quite unable to concentrate on his food, or even find time to cultivate his indignation at the insultingly remote table assigned to him at the very back of the room. The time had really come to tell Mansur where his duty lay. Sonny regretted that his chances of evading capture would be somewhat reduced by committing murder on live television, but the poetic justice of a public execution easily outweighed the almost certain loss of a faithful retainer. With great foresight Auntie had made Mansur bring a small picnic hamper in case the Elysian food turned out to be unsuitable. The main course of Beef Wellington could hardly have been more unsuitable for the Hindu party, and Mansur gradually distributed the contents of the creaking wicker hamper that nestled discreetly on the floor next to a fire extinguisher and a bright red bucket of sand.

'Sonny!' said Auntie, clasping his forearm, as if her chair alone couldn't be expected to provide enough support under these conditions. 'You'll never guess what's happened.'

'I give up,' said Sonny, still scanning the entrance in the hope of seeing Craig arrive.

'The Russian gentleman to my right, who is the owner of the famous Page and Turner, has commissioned a memoir from me, all about the old days in Badanpur, before Independence and Partition: the glamour, the Durbars, the purdah, and the disastrous advent of modern India, Mrs Gandhi's betrayal of the Constitutional guarantees offered to the princely states . . . are you all right?'

Sonny, who had inhaled a pickled walnut on first hearing the news of Yuri's commission, was bent double with a napkin pressed to his mouth, trying to

muffle the coughing fit that shook his prodigious
frame and flushed his face with blood.

'Now, look here,' said Malcolm into the emergency
phone, 'I don't want to be told to press the ground-
floor button again, we've been through all that. I
want you to send us a lift engineer immediately.'

Malcolm listened for a while to the reply.

'Where exactly are you?' he asked suspiciously. 'In
Bhopal? Well, what earthly use are you to someone
stuck in a lift in London?'

David took another swing at the doors with his
walking stick.

'Please stop that,' snapped Malcolm. 'No, not
you. I have someone in the lift with me who suffers
from acute claustrophobia. Hello? Hello?'

Malcolm hung up the emergency phone with an
exasperated sigh, and took his own phone out of his
breast pocket.

'Oh, Christ, I haven't got a signal.'

'Don't panic,' said David, 'I have one of these
satellite phones – they're frightfully expensive, but
they work pretty well anywhere. The colonel of the

SAS is a friend of mine and I happen to know that he's dining in London tonight.'

'Isn't that going a bit far?' said Malcolm. 'What we really need is a lift engineer.'

'In an emergency always go straight to the top,' said David firmly. 'There's no point in cutting corners.'

'What direction do you see yourself taking the prize in?' Jo asked Mr Wo, in a combative tone that suggested she was ready to fight any answer he gave, so it was no use trying to guess what she wanted to hear.

'It's a prize for literature,' said Mr Wo. 'I hope it will go in the direction of literature. My wife takes a great interest in these things. Personally I think that competition should be encouraged in war and sport and business, but that it makes no sense in the arts. If an artist is good, nobody else can do what he or she does and therefore all comparisons are incoherent. Only the mediocre, pushing forward a commonplace view of life in a commonplace language, can really be compared, but my wife thinks that "least mediocre of the mediocre" is a discouraging title for a prize,' Mr Wo couldn't help laughing.

Jo didn't know where to begin. She disagreed with everything that Mr Wo had said, as well as with the assumptions behind everything he had said, but she was temporarily paralysed by the abundance of potential targets. Her hesitation gave Mr Wo the chance to speak again.

'I am a little concerned,' he said cheerfully, 'our panna cotta with mixed woodland berries is about to arrive and there is still no sign of the chairman.'

'I'm more than happy to take over,' said Jo.

'No need,' said Mr Wo, 'Tobias has already offered to "step up to the plate" – a baseball metaphor, I believe, which even your prime minister has started to favour over the "wicket", such is the British enthusiasm for the Special Relationship.'

Jo stared incredulously at Tobias, who was leaning towards Penny, listening carefully to what she was saying.

'Excuse me,' said a timid voice behind Jo.

'Yes.'

'I'm Robin Wentworth, the author of *The Enigma Conundrum*. I just wanted to take the opportunity of thanking you personally for putting me on the Short List.'

'No need to thank me,' said Jo, 'your advocate

was Penny Feathers. Why don't you go and interrupt her. She looks to me as if she's conspiring to pervert the course of justice.'

'Congratulations on your Short Listing,' said Mr Wo, shaking hands with Robin Wentworth. 'As you can see, tempers run high among the judges. You could do us all a great favour by finding Malcolm Craig and Sir David Hampshire; we seem to have lost them.'

'I have an idea,' said Robin eagerly, 'I saw them downstairs.'

'Proper little boy scout,' said Jo, as he set off.

'Excuse me,' said Mr Wo, 'I must have a word with my wife.'

'But you do realize,' said Jo, 'that we haven't made a final decision yet.'

'Yes,' said Mr Wo, 'Penny explained everything. Maybe I will ask Vanessa if she could compromise a little.'

'Hello!' said Malcolm, spreading his arms to encompass the table. 'I'm so sorry, we've been trapped in the lift. I do apologize, Mr Wo, Mrs Wo, all of you. It was a bit of a nightmare, especially for poor David.

Just as we were about to despair, and David was on his satellite phone to a friend in the SAS, we were saved by one of the Short Listees. Naturally, we'd been pushing all the buttons we could lay our hands on, but for some reason he was able to call the lift from the first floor. It's the strongest argument I've heard for including a thriller writer on the Short List. You wouldn't find the author of *The Frozen Torrent* showing that sort of initiative.'

Malcolm glanced over to see the effect of his barb on Vanessa, but she was absorbed in listening to Mr Wo.

'Sorry, but Tobias won't budge,' said Penny, leaning over to Malcolm. 'He's in a hate because when we couldn't find you, Mr Wo asked him to stand in, and he's spent the whole of dinner composing an "utterly brilliant" speech.'

'Christ!' said Malcolm. 'He's only ever attended one meeting! I suppose I'll have to announce joint winners.'

'Please sit down,' said Mrs Wo to David, 'you must be exhausted. What did your army friend say when you rang from the lift?'

'He told me,' said David, pausing to take a gulp of water, 'to bugger off and call an engineer.'

'Oh, dear, how unfortunate,' said Mrs Wo, with a perfectly judged laugh that contained no mockery, only relief and sympathy.

'I must get something inside me before my speech,' said Malcolm.

'No hurry,' said Mrs Wo, 'you have eighteen minutes. Perhaps some dessert and a small glass of wine.'

'Quickest way to raise the old blood sugar,' said Malcolm, knocking back a glass of wine and working his way swiftly through a little tub of panna cotta and woodland berries.

The prospect of being on national television, and having three or four minutes of it exclusively to himself – longer than a prime minister on the news during a major crisis – which in some ways, or more precisely, in every way, had been Malcolm's motivation for accepting the job as chairman of the Elysian Prize, was now turning into a persecution and a potential source of humiliation. He had written a speech with two possible endings, one printed in green for the victory of *wot u starin at* and one written in red for the victory of *The Palace Cookbook*. Now he would have to improvise a merger of these two endings and present the resulting train wreck as some kind of cultural triumph. He quickly devoured a second panna cotta, abandoned by Penny during her negotiations with Tobias.

Mr Wo was about to ask Malcolm for a quiet word, when a woman with a belt full of brushes approached and said it was time to do his make-up.

'Just a moment,' said Malcolm, hoping Wo had some good news.

'We can't discuss this – for obvious reasons,' said Mr Wo, smiling and tilting his head discreetly towards the television camera aimed at them across the table. 'Apparently, the broadcaster employs lip-readers in case someone indiscreetly names the winner in public.'

'I understand,' said Malcolm, smiling back at him while accepting an envelope.

'I finally persuaded Vanessa to commit.'

'Thank God for that,' said Malcolm.

He couldn't look inside until he was out of range of the cameras, and the moment he left the Banqueting Room, the make-up artist immediately sat Malcolm down in the corridor and started to pat his face with a sponge and then dust it with a soft brush. He instinctively closed his eyes, holding the envelope tightly in his lap.

'I'm sure that'll be fine,' he said impatiently.

'Almost finished,' said the make-up artist, but as soon as she had stepped back to admire her work, a young woman with a walkie-talkie came over and said, 'Three minutes.'

'I really must have some time to myself,' said Malcolm, 'to . . .' he hesitated to say 'find out who's won' and so he settled on 'gather my resources'.

'I completely understand,' said the young woman. 'Don't forget to breathe slowly.'

'Why?'

'It helps you to relax.'

'I don't need to relax! I just need a moment *alone*,' said Malcolm.

'I totally understand, I'll leave you now and come back in about two minutes.'

Vanessa suddenly couldn't bear it any longer. She knew that she had voted out of spite and anger and she felt ashamed of herself.

'Excuse me,' she said to David Hampshire, who was about to repeat the crushing remark he had made to the Spanish ambassador after he claimed that Britain was nothing but 'a small island clinging to small islands'.

Vanessa hurried towards the door she had seen Malcolm go through. Out in the corridor she spotted him sitting on a chair, next to a temporary control centre, with a console of dials and knobs being checked by two men in headphones. As Vanessa approached, a young woman with a walkie-talkie blocked her path.

'I'm sorry but this area is restricted during the broadcast,' she said.

'But I have to speak to Malcolm Craig,' said Vanessa.

'He's specifically asked to be alone. I'm afraid you'll have to talk to him after the announcement.'

'But I'm on the committee,' said Vanessa. 'He's about to make the wrong announcement.'

'I very much doubt that,' said the young woman, 'he's the chair of the judges and whoever you are, I'm quite sure he knows more about what's going on than you do. Now, I'm going to have to ask you to leave, please.'

Vanessa did not move, but a man with ginger hair and a black T-shirt came over and said, 'One minute,' to the woman with the walkie-talkie.

'Okay, I'm going to take him in. Could you accompany this lady back to the Banqueting Room?'

'Malcolm!' Vanessa cried out in despair, but when he glanced in her direction, Malcolm looked straight through her and continued towards the door that led to the far end of the Banqueting Room.

Watching Malcolm labour up the steps to the stage, Penny was assailed by guilt and anxiety. Why had she ever encouraged Nicola to place a bet? Vanessa had disappeared before Penny had time to find out her final decision, and Mr Wo refused to 'spoil the surprise' by telling her the result. Fingers crossed all would be well, but if things didn't go her way, Penny's moral dilemma was whether to refund Nicola's original bet, or refund the sum Nicola would have won if Penny had provided her with an accurate tip. Perhaps she could get away with not refunding her at all. A gamble was a gamble, after all.

As Malcolm arrived on the stage, he paused a moment to allow the toastmaster to do his job.

"Your Excellencies, my Lords, Ladies and Gentlemen, pray silence for the Right Honourable Malcolm Craig, MP, Chair of the 2013 Elysian Prize.'

Malcolm spread his speech on the lectern, and put

on his reading glasses with an air of unhurried self-assurance, smiling at the room he assumed was still there, although it was lost in the glare of the television lights. He had already been feeling a strange disquiet as he climbed to the stage, something much more menacing than the familiar strain of public speaking; now that he had to begin his speech, there was a surge in the strength of his anxiety. He could hear a high-pitched humming in his ears, and his body was throbbing, as if it had become a kettledrum for his pounding heart. What was going on? An electric tingling washed over his skin and he wondered if he was about to faint. With self-fulfilling dread he realized that he was experiencing stage fright for the first time. He had spent his professional life queuing up for a presidential slice of airtime, but now that he had what he thought he wanted, it felt like a primal threat to his existence.

'I used to think,' he began, knowing these were the opening words of his speech, but when he looked down at the page he felt utterly disconnected from the text in front of him.

The hall remained silent, apart from a few coughs and some ill-mannered conversation from people who weren't even pretending to listen.

'With a product as varied and flexible and, eh, slippery as the novel,' Malcolm improvised, 'there's nothing to grab hold of.' He clutched the podium, feeling that everyone knew that he was really talking about his vertigo and expected him to fall over at any moment.

'You can talk about relevance,' he said, grateful to Jo for the first time since he'd met her, 'or, um, the human condition, or . . . eh, style, yes, writing style; but in the end it's all a matter of personal taste.'

Malcolm could hear himself stumbling from one platitude to another, but there was nothing he could do beyond hoping to survive. What was it in his nature that destroyed these moments of potential triumph? Why had he made his fatal speech about Scottish independence when he appeared to be rising inexorably toward a cabinet post? Why had he proposed to two women on the same day and in the ensuing muddle lost both of them, although they had both accepted? Why had he not declared his interest in *The Greasy Pole* when the committee was considering it? He couldn't think about it now, that flaw that made him throw away the game at the last moment. The one thing he knew was that he must stop talking about writing. Anything he said might be taken down and used by the press when they exposed the *Greasy Pole* scandal. He glanced up and thought he could make out figures twitching over their phones. The story was probably breaking as he spoke, appearing on people's screens around the room, and being discussed by the pundits back in the studio.

'What we have offered the public is the opinions of five judges who were all asking themselves the same basic question: "Which one of these books could be enjoyed by the largest number of ordinary people up and down this country?" '

How many times had he used that phrase in his political career? He was close to tears at the thought, but powerless to say anything meaningful.

'When a journalist asked me what qualifications I had for this job . . .'

Why had he said that? He was like a criminal returning to the scene of his crime.

'What I told him was that I'd taken my lessons from the best teachers of all: the British people.'

Flatter the audience, always works.

'Now, if you would prefer to trust the opinion of one journalist who sets himself up as judge and jury and executioner for the entire prize, without having read all two hundred books we ploughed our way through, then be my guest.'

Oh, God, the good old combative approach.

'Before I make the final announcement, I want to thank my fellow judges for their . . . for their passionate dedication to the cause of literature. I'm quite sure that we shall remain friends, reminiscing fondly about the ups and downs of the selection process in the years to come.

'I would also like to thank Sir David Hampshire, in the year of his retirement. David has been the power behind the prize, always close to hand, ready to smooth ruffled feathers, and offer the wisdom he draws from his vast wealth of experience.'

Malcolm paused in vain for a round of applause.

'And so, without further ado,' he resumed, impulsively deciding that the public could do without any praise of the Short-Listed books or explanation of the committee's final choice, 'the winner of the 2013 Elysian Prize is *The Palace Cookbook* by Lakshmi Badanpur.'

John Elton snapped the stem of his wine glass.

Jo smiled triumphantly at Vanessa's empty seat.

LOST FOR WORDS

Alan stared down the well shaft of his empty panna-cotta ramekin.

Penny decided that ultimately it was not her responsibility if Nicola chose to gamble with her savings, but that she would chip in something towards a new roof.

Auntie let out a cry of unfeigned consternation. Camera lights were soon shining in her eyes and everyone at her table pressing forward to offer their congratulations. Yuri expressed his joy while reminding Auntie that she was under contract to Page and Turner.

'Of course,' she murmured, 'my memoir . . . Oh, Sonny, I'm not sure I can manage.'

'Of course you can. Remember who you are!'

'I do remember who I am, but I don't remember being a writer. Ah, Mansur, there you are. Please help me up, I'm feeling a little dizzy. Where have you been?'

'I was near the stage, ready to do my duty; then I heard that your Highness had won and . . .'

'Never mind all that,' said Sonny.

'Do his duty – what an earth does he mean?'

'Auntie, you're needed at the front!'

To Sonny's relief, a young woman with a walkie-talkie came up to Auntie.

'Could you please come to the podium as quickly as possible, Lakshmi? We've cut to our panel of critics in the studio, but we've got the news coming up in twenty minutes, and obviously everyone is very keen to hear your speech.'

'I only wish I were very keen to make it,' said Auntie, 'but to tell you the truth, I'm dreading it. Where is Didier? Oh, Didier, it was so kind of you to write that speech for me, but I'm not sure I completely understand it.'

'Excellent!' said Didier. 'If you understood it, no doubt you would disagree, but this way you can deliver it with perfect sincerity!'

Not entirely reassured, Auntie was led past dozens of tables where the words 'absurd' and 'ridiculous' seemed to be playing an unusually large part in the conversation. By the time she reached the lectern, she was so anxious that she wondered if she would be able to speak at all.

'What is literature?' she began, feeling that her voice was not her own. 'What is this privilege we grant to certain verbal combinations, although they employ the very same words we use to buy our bread and count our money? Words are our slaves: they may be used to fetch a pair of slippers, or to build the great pyramid of Giza: they depend on syntax to make the order of the world manifest, to raise stones into arches and arches into aqueducts.

'*The Palace Cookbook* forces the recognition of this truth through the play of irony and absence: the only authentic relationship modernity can have with the classical ideals of equilibrium and lucidity. By appearing to use language for the most banal purpose, for the maintenance of our material existence through eating, we are thrown into a crisis of meaning. Is this all there is to life? And yet slowly, through the hypnotic reiteration of quantities and ingredients: rice, water, flour, oil, ounces, pounds, cups and teaspoons, the author invokes, through their absence, the impossible ambitions of the highest art. Right from the beginning, in the title itself and in the Introduction, we are in the presence of this paradox. The Palace, we are told, is ruined, abandoned, lost, and yet it stands behind the Cookbook, just as the matrix of syntax stands behind the banality of the semantic corpus, ready to transform it into the scandal of excess and transgression of utility that is art!

'When Foucault tells us, in *The Order of Things* . . .'

Auntie couldn't go on. She had no idea what Didier was driving at and felt that, whatever the consequences, she must tell the truth.

'Ladies and gentlemen,' she resumed, 'I want to thank Monsieur Didier Leroux for writing me such a clever speech and trying to make me a worthy recipient of this famous literary prize, but I have to say that I am a simple woman and that what I set out to do when I wrote *The Palace Cookbook* was to record as many recipes as possible before they were irrevocably lost. These recipes have been passed down from head cook to head cook over the centuries, but never written down, being treated as a kind of secret family knowledge. Fortunately we were able to interview the last cook, Babu Singh, a few months before he died. Despite being very old and completely blind, Babu had a perfect recall of the recipes and was able to recite them like verses, day after day for a week. The way of life that accompanied those dishes has gone for ever – the tiger hunts, the elephant fights, the stables with a hundred matching polo ponies, the six hundred household staff, and the very special relationship between a maharaja and his people, who looked to him as children look to their father: for kindness and advice. The palaces have fallen into disrepair, or been turned into hotels – but I hoped that perhaps I could bring the culinary art perfected over many generations to a more varied world, and preserve some of the splendour of that tradition by sharing it more widely.

'Mr Malcolm Craig has told us that the novel is such a "varied" and "flexible" form, and yet no one could be more amazed than I am to discover that I have transformed my cookery book into a work of literature, simply by including one or two stories about some of our more colourful ancestors.

'I want to thank the distinguished panel of judges for giving me this prize, and to say that I shall donate the money to the Badanpur Orphanage, of which I have the honour to be the Patron.'

Auntie bowed to her audience and crossed the stage with quiet dignity, holding her sari a little raised as she walked cautiously down the steps, amidst a scattering of applause, tentative in places and fanatically enthusiastic in others.

'Fucking hell,' said Katherine, staring at the television from her bed, while Sam stared at her glowing skin from the pillow beside her, 'that's the book that Alan sent to the judges instead of *Consequences*.'

'The world's gone mad,' said Sam, leaning over to kiss her on the neck.

'Listen to *this*,' said Katherine. 'It's an interview with one of the judges' daughters.'

Sam turned to the screen and saw an angry-looking, middle-aged woman standing in front of a terraced house, with her arms folded across a thick sweater.

'Yes, I'm saying that my mother told me to place a bet on *wot u starin at*. She gave me inside information and encouraged me to commit what would in effect have been fraud.'

'But it wasn't fraud, was it, because that book didn't win?'

'That doesn't mean she didn't try to cheat,' said Nicola stubbornly, 'it's just another thing she isn't any good at.'

'Great,' said Sam, relighting the joint. 'Maybe there'll be a retrial and we can both get Short-Listed and one of us can win. I don't mind which one of us, that's how madly in love I am.'

'If you were madly in love, you'd want me to win,' said Katherine.

'I'm not sure that's true,' said Sam. 'I think love is about equality: both of us equally happy with either result. One-sided self-sacrifice is only enabling some-one else's egoism. Altruists always end up riddled with resentment, or if they make that last superhuman effort, with spiritual pride.'

'Oh,' said Katherine, 'you mean you're not going to enable my egoism.'

'Okay, okay,' said Sam 'you're right – love is doing everything you want all the time.'

'Only because you want it too,' said Katherine.

'Hmm, the ever-popular merged volition,' said Sam, 'that can work, for about three weeks.'

'Oh, look,' said Katherine, lying down sideways, with her head in her hand, 'it's the mother of that woman.'

Sam looked at Katherine, her fine shoulder blades, the line of her waist, the ridge of her hipbone, and her legs tapering into the sheets.

'Amazing,' he said.

'She's been told about her daughter,' said Katherine.

Sam looked back up at the television. Penny was still in the Banqueting Room, with the empty stage behind her.

'I have no idea why she would say something like

that. Nicola has always been fond of a practical joke, but I really think this is going a bit too far. Besides, it makes no sense, since the book I'm *supposed* to have recommended didn't win!'

'She says that's just incompetence,' said the interviewer. 'Were you planning to share the money?'

'Now, look here,' said Penny, genuinely indignant, 'our committee has been working extremely hard all year, in order to bring the very best works of literature to the public's attention, and those discussions have always been *strictly confidential*. To suggest otherwise is not only an insult to me but also to my colleagues and friends.'

'Some of us have been following Jo Cross's Twitter wars with critics of the Long List for several weeks now,' said the interviewer.

'I'm not prepared to discuss these matters any further,' said Penny, 'for the very reason that they are, as I've said, strictly confidential.'

'Are you saying that Twitter is confidential?'

Penny turned her back on the camera and walked out of shot.

'Oh dear, well, I seem to have lost Penny Feathers,' said the interviewer. 'I suspect we'll be hearing a lot more about this year's highly controversial Elysian

Prize, but that's all we've got time for tonight and so . . .'

Katherine switched off the television and tossed the remote control onto the floor under her bedside table.

'I'm sick of prizes,' she said.

'Comparison, competition, envy and anxiety,' said Sam.

'Let's just make love and be happy.'

'*Vaste Programme*,' said Sam, 'as De Gaulle said to the heckler who shouted, "Death to the idiots".'

'That *is* too ambitious,' said Katherine, 'but my programme is completely realistic, especially the first half.'

'Ah, the first half,' said Sam, sliding down the sheets.

'Which will lead naturally to the second half,' said Katherine.

They smiled at each other and all the irony seemed to have rushed from the world, restoring it to a place where things happened naturally and incomparably.